Trapped in Mirrors

How the Luckiest Man in the World Became a Spy

A Novel Based on True Events

Michael Connick

Copyright © 2016 Michael Connick

All rights reserved. No part of this book may be reproduced, stored in a retrieval system, or transmitted in any form or by any means without prior written permission, except in the case of brief quotations embodied in articles or reviews.

ISBN: 1523422777
ISBN-13: 978-1523422777

4th Printing

DEDICATION

To my dear friends: whether near, far, or gone forever – you have all changed me for the better. Thanks Beau, Greg, Harry, Amy, Ralph, and John.

To my children, Wendy and Stephen, who live far away from me on another coast - I love you both and think of you constantly. May your lives be filled with success and joy.

CONTENTS

	Acknowledgments	i
1	Prologue	1
2	How It All Began	5
3	NSA – The Great Puzzle Palace	15
4	Starting My New Job	20
5	My Science Fiction Project Finally Revealed	26
6	Onward, Upward, and Outward	31
7	Off to Tehran	42
8	I Really Put My Foot In It	55
9	The People Become Unsettled	63
10	Home Sweet Home	69
11	Off to Vienna	83
12	The Truth Finally Revealed	96
13	Things Get Interesting	110
14	The KGB Pitches a Fit and I Take a Train Ride	120
15	The Investigation Drags On and On	129
16	Boy, You're Not Going to Believe What Happened to Me	136
17	The Shit Hits the Fan	142
18	My Triumphant Return	149

19	Epilogue	155
	About the Author	158

ACKNOWLEDGMENTS

This book would not have been written without the encouragement of my wonderful wife, Gloria. I would never have begun writing it, nor working to have it actually published, without her continual support and complete confidence in me. Thank you, my dearest!

This book would be filled with typos and punctuation errors, if not for the heroic proofreading efforts of my dear friend Amy. My most heartfelt thanks to you, Amy!

Finally, to my docent friend Len, who had the courage to make just one more final pass through this book, and slayed the last minor nits in it. Thanks, Len!

1

PROLOGUE

Today, I sit on my living room couch in the quiet little town of Huntington, West Virginia. I've been retired for almost a year. I've just finished a very satisfying breakfast with my new wife, with whom I've been married for a little over a year. Our house is still filled with the smell of cooked bacon. Life here is wonderful in its slowness and simplicity, especially after a frantic lifetime of demanding work and near continuous travel. I used to spend more time in hotels or temporary apartments than at home, and so I now enjoy the cozy atmosphere here that my wife has so expertly and effortlessly created for us. The warm sun is streaming in through the window and an old clock chimes the quarter hour. We are very comfortable here. Sitting contentedly with a computer on my lap I guess I now feel compelled to share a portion of my personal history with you, dear reader. It was so very, very different from what it is now.

My name is Stephen Connor. I think the most interesting part of my life, the part I'm going to tell you about in this book, occurred between the years of 1968 and 1982 – 14 years during which I worked at some pretty unusual jobs within the US intelligence community. These jobs took me across the US, off to the Middle East, to a very beautiful part of Europe, and back home again. Actually the term "intelligence community" is somewhat ironic as it's hard to view it as anything close to a real community. A group of angry two year-olds would be a more accurate picture of the relationships within this "community".

I first worked for the National Security Agency (NSA), and then was very unexpectedly transferred to the Central Intelligence Agency (CIA). Although both of these organizations are concerned with safeguarding our country from external threats, at the time I worked for them they seemed to spend most of their energies in inter-mural squabbles with each other. That's what made this transfer so inexplicable to me at first. The only organization they hated more than each other was the Defense Intelligence Agency (DIA). Well, that's another story – one beyond what I'll be covering in this book.

During my time with both of these organizations I first started worked in bleeding-edge technology initiatives utilizing computers. However, I eventually ended up stumbling into a real life "spy" role with the CIA. Although I'm about as far away from a James Bond-like character as you can imagine, I actually managed to blunder completely by accident into some very real life-threatening situations. I incurred the wrath of the KGB and became the target of a psychopathic killer. Through a lot of luck and a little bit of guile, I managed to not only survive these incidents, but to actually succeed as a CIA clandestine agent, and it all happened pretty much by accident. That's the story I want to tell you about in this little book. Of course, I'll first have to start off with some pretty mundane material to show you exactly how I managed to end up in these strange and perilous predicaments. Let's start right now.

2

HOW IT ALL BEGAN

I was an only-child born and raised in San Francisco. My father was born there, too. We had even gone to the same high school: Lowell High. It was the only non-district high school in the city and was really something of a public college prep school. All the brainy kids went there and I was definitely a brainy, nerdy kid. My mother was an English war bride, brought home by my father after World War II ended. Like my father, she was very intelligent but much stronger willed than he was. All of us were voracious readers and our home was filled with books.

I was a tall and skinny kid and had brown hair and brown eyes. I was gawky and very non-athletic, a bookworm and very shy. I seemed to stumble a lot over the tiniest things on the ground. My mother's goal for me was to win a Nobel Prize and during the awards ceremony say: "This is all because of you, mom!"

My dad just loved me for who I was and just wanted me to be happy in life. It seemed natural that I should go to the same college that he did. He had been quite an athlete, but I was the antithesis. I could not accurately throw, hit, or catch any type of ball. Somehow, my dad never seemed to mind and still loved me anyway.

It was 1968 and I was about to graduate from San Francisco State College. 1968 was a tumultuous year of protests. Draft card burnings were becoming common. Martin Luther King was assassinated in April. It was also the beginning of the Troubles in Northern Ireland and the Prague Spring behind the Iron Curtain in Czechoslovakia. Johnny Cash performed his famous concert in Folsom Prison, and the Who, Jimmy Hendrix, The Beatles, and the Yardbirds were all over the radio airwaves. In May, Buffalo Springfield would perform together for the last time. Woodstock was still a year away.

I left home and lived in Haight-Asbury during my college years, not because I was a hippy but because I thought mere proximity to all of those hippies would somehow make me a lot cooler. There was also plentiful pot there and the promise of free love. Anyway, by 1968 the Summer of Love was winding down and all the real hippies seemed to be heading off to communes. Speed freaks and heroin addicts, many of who carried guns and knives instead of love beads, were slowly replacing them. It was starting to get a little dark in this part of town and I was actually looking forward to leaving it for someplace more peaceful.

I lived on the third floor of a somewhat rundown four-story apartment house. I had a view of what is called the Panhandle of Golden Gate Park – the three-quarters of a mile long and one block wide appendage that sticks out of the eastern side of the main park. Since San Francisco was a city without real seasons, the whole park was always lush and green and I loved my view of it. I lived within walking distance of my grandparents' apartment just on the other side of the Panhandle. I could still remember feeding squirrels there with my father and grandfather when I was very young. It was a magic place full of wonderful memories for me.

The southern side of the Panhandle where I lived was really the wrong side of the tracks – where all those hippies lived. My apartment house was full of them, and they certainly seemed to be free of societal restraints, but not all that happy. One young man was about to be evicted after he had fried his brain from too much LSD. Another young girl killed herself there by slashing her wrists in her bathroom.

Haight Street was in the process of turning into a real zoo. Tour buses crept down this street on weekends filled with tourists from Kansas marveling at the savages running loose right before their eyes. The street was full of "head shops" offering over-priced souvenirs of the hippy lifestyle to tourists brave enough to get off the bus. Nobody who actually lived in Haight-Asbury could afford their prices.

If you walked down the street and were younger than thirty ("Never trust anyone over thirty!"), you were guaranteed to be approached by someone dressed like a magazine writer's concept of a hippie. They would surreptitiously whisper "Grass?" to you. This was one of the many rip-off artists who now preyed on young tourists eager to have a little excitement in their lives. These tourists wanted to really experience, for the very first time, what it was like to get high. If they engaged the conman in conversation, he would offer them a large quantity of some absolutely amazing marijuana at a fairly reasonable price.

"Just give me the money and I'll be right back with the good stuff," he would croon to the excited victim. After the money changed hands, it would be: "I'll be right back, don't move." Then he would disappear into a building, go out the back way, and it would take some time for the poor chump to realize that he'd been swindled. Then what could he do – call the cops? It was getting to be a very mean street, indeed.

A few of the other "hippies" living in my apartment house were actually struggling college students like me. They might also be free from societal restraints, but they still had to please their professors. I did have one professor who was more of a hippie than any of us pretended to be. The first day of his class, he came in wearing long hair tied back with a red bandana, a leather fringed jacket, tie-died t-shirt, jeans with an Indian-beaded belt, and cowboy boots. He stood up in front of the class and gave us a rousing speech.

He said: "Fellow humans, I utterly reject the unjust system of grades that the fascist administration of this oppressive institution is trying to impose upon you. So, every one of you will receive an 'A' from me no matter what you do in this class. In fact, if you have something better to do at this time of day, I urge you to go do it. Do not fall into the grade slavery trap!"

With that, I left his class never to return. I actually did get an 'A' from him. He was a very cool dude and he must have had tenure.

Of course, there was a huge black cloud hovering over my otherwise carefree college years. It was that darned inconvenient conflict – the Vietnam War. It darkened my horizons whenever I thought about life after college. Graduation was normally supposed to lead to a wonderful future of interesting pursuits and opportunities for earning a fat salary. Yet there it stood before me, this horrible monster that was sucking up America's youth and spitting them out into nasty rice paddies in Southeast Asia. Everyone I knew was opposed to this war and there certainly seemed to be no glory to be gained by participating in it. My college deferment was about to end and the draft boards continued to have a ravenous appetite for young men just like me. What the hell was I going to do?

Like all young men during this time, it seemed to come down to a very small set of remarkably unattractive choices:

1. I could just wait to be drafted and hope for the best.
2. I could enlist in some branch of service that promised to send me to a locale more hospitable than Vietnam - say like Korea.
3. I could flee the country for Canada, or some other country that sheltered draft dodgers, and completely give up my life in the US.

Choice 3 was definitely out, but 1 and 2 both looked pretty unattractive as well.

Then a miracle happened. My Russian professor, Dr. Bazhenov, approached me and inquired as to my plans for dealing with the draft. He really looked the part of a Russian professor, complete with a Van Dyke beard. I thought he looked a lot like Lenin, but never dared to tell him that. He seemed completely humorless.

He asked: "So, Mr. Connor, are you planning on enlisting or waiting to be drafted after graduation?"

"I have absolutely no idea what I'm going to do," I replied.

"Well, because of your very somewhat unusual academic background I may have an alternative option for you. Would you be open to it?"

"Absolutely," I replied very enthusiastically.

Before continuing to describe this conversation, I should let you know just what my "somewhat unusual academic background" was. By the time I had entered college I had decided to become a lawyer. I was a pretty bright kid and loved to argue, so it seemed like the perfect career for me. However, I was also an extreme nerd at heart. I loved science and I loved math. Also, for some unknown reason, I really enjoyed learning foreign languages. This enjoyment for learning languages never seemed to be matched by any great ability to actually master them, but that never stopped me from trying. So, in high school I had taken two years of French. In college I studied Russian for two years. I was the only student at San Francisco State that I knew of that majored in Political Science, an excellent pre-law major, and minored in Math, thus satisfying my nerd cravings. In addition, I was one of the few students who had any proficiency at all in both French and Russian.

Dr. Bazhenov continued, "I believe I can set up an interview for you with some gentlemen who will discuss an interesting opportunity. It would come with a deferment from military service. Of course, you will have to cut your hair and clean up your act a bit. Also, if you have been taking any drugs you will need to be completely truthful with them about it. If you attempt to deceive them about any aspect of your life, this opportunity will be lost to you forever. What do you say?"

I had really only smoked grass in college, although a fair amount of it. I certainly would be more than happy to cut my hair, which was long enough to be tied back into a very nice looking ponytail. I was also willing to drop the paisley dashiki and bell-bottom pants I often wore for something much more square. I was willing to make all these sacrifices and even more in order to have a chance of not fighting in a rice paddy. Heck, I'd get a crew cut and shave off my beard if necessary!

"Please, Dr. Bazhenov, set up the interview as soon as you can. I'm very interested!"

So, that's exactly what he did. In mid-May of 1968, just a month before I was scheduled to graduate, I found myself in a nondescript office building on Market Street in downtown San Francisco sitting in front of two men. They both sat in old-fashion wooden chairs behind an ornate wooden table. I sat before them in a rather uncomfortable wooden chair that seemed pretty beat up and worn out. The whole office reminded me of Sam Spade's office in the "Maltese Falcon".

I had a neatly trimmed beard, a very conservative haircut, and wore slacks, dress shirt, and black shiny Oxford shoes. I almost didn't recognize myself when I had glanced in a mirror that morning before leaving for my interview. I looked like a narc!

One of the two men sitting before me definitely appeared to be a military type. He sat stiffly erect in his chair and was quite muscular. He had very close-cropped blonde hair and what I can only describe as steely gray eyes. Yes, it's a cliché, but they really looked like that to me. He wore gray dress pants, a white shirt and black skinny tie, and a gray sports jacket with very small dark blue checks. His intense stare actually made me feel uncomfortable. He introduced himself as Bill.

His companion was almost the opposite in type. He looked more like a salesman than a military man. He said his name was John. He wore an expensive looking dark blue suit, a pale blue shirt, and a bright red power tie. He smiled a lot. He smelled of cologne. Maybe he was the Joel Cairo of this Maltese Falcon-themed meeting.

Bill spoke first: "Before we begin I would like you to look over and sign the brief document I'm about to give you. It basically says that you promise not to discuss anything regarding this interview, even with your parents or your most trusted friends. Unless you are willing to sign it and fully comply with it, this interview will now end."

Well, that was interesting. I had guessed that I was interviewing for some kind of government job, maybe as a translator of some type, but this hinted at something a bit more sinister. Nevertheless I took the document, quickly glanced through it, and promptly signed it. I wasn't even deterred by the phrases within the document that referred to criminal prosecution if I violated any of the terms contained within it.

After handing the signed document back to Bill, I asked: "Can I get a copy of this?"

"No," was his very succinct reply.

He stuffed the document into a leather briefcase at his side and turned to John. "Let's get started," he said.

In spite of looking like a salesman, when John finally spoke it was in a very precise and formal manner. "Mr. Connor, we have a proposition for you that I hope you will find interesting. We want to offer you a job, really a very interesting and challenging career, which we think you may enjoy immensely. It is a job with an agency of the United States government and as such will offer you a deferment from military service. You will be living and working in the mid-Atlantic area of the United States. You will be paid a reasonable salary and will be provided with excellent benefits. You will also be providing a valuable service to your country. What do you think about this proposal?"

I said: "I'm very interested, please continue."

He did: "We have spoken with Dr. Bazhenov and other of your instructors at San Francisco State. They all speak very highly of your intelligence. We are also very interested in the somewhat unusual choice of courses that you've taken there. We feel that all of this makes you particularly qualified for the position we have in mind for you. I do have one question for you though: have you ever done any work with computers?"

Now remember, this was 1968. The computers of the time were primarily giant mainframes that filled huge climate controlled rooms. The rooms had false floors covering miles of electrical cables connecting all of the various computer components. To my knowledge, San Francisco State only had one fairly old computer on its campus at that time, and the only computer courses offered there were within the Electronic Engineering Department. These mainly dealt with computer hardware design. The whole domain of software engineering and systems analysis was in its very infancy then. Even the largest super-computers of this era had less computing power than you now possess in your smartphone.

I had never taken a computer course of any kind and didn't have any practical experience with computers. My general interest in all things scientific had led me to some reading regarding computers, but my knowledge was actually quite scant and I admitted that to John.

"That's all right," he said. "You can be trained in all the necessary skills. In fact, it may even be advantageous that you won't have to unlearn anything that might interfere with your progress in mastering the skills you will need to perform this job. Your math skills will certainly help. May I ask if you have any interest at all in computers?"

"Yes, certainly. What little I do know about them I find fascinating." Maybe just a slight exaggeration, but it was what I thought they wanted to hear.

"Excellent," said John. "I really feel that we have a great fit between your background, aptitudes, and the requirements of this position. Bill, would you like to take over now?"

Bill grunted acceptance and pulled out some papers from inside his briefcase. "I would like you to fill out these forms, please. I need to warn you that you will have to be completely honest and forthcoming in all your responses. They will all be independently verified and any dishonesty will not only disqualify you from the job we are considering offering you, but may also subject you to criminal prosecution. Do you understand?"

This was getting seriously weird, but I quickly agreed. He handed me a thick stack of forms. "We will leave you to fill these out. We will return in an hour. Would you like some coffee or anything else to drink?"

I said: "Some coffee would be great." They both left the room and Bill returned shortly with a mug of coffee. "We'll be back in an hour. Please don't leave this room until we return and be sure to fill out all of the forms we've given you as completely as you can. We will answer any questions you may have regarding them when we return." With that he left and closed the door behind him. I waited a few minutes until I was sure they were gone and tried the doorknob. Sure enough, it was locked. I was locked in until they returned. I sincerely hoped that no fire would break out in the building before then!

Oh well, onto the forms. All they did was ask me about every facet of my life up until that day. They also wanted to know all about my family members – who they were, where they were born, how old they were, where they lived now, etc.

The most fascinating form to me concerned my education. It asked me to list every single school I'd ever attended, when I had attended them, and the names of all of my teachers from kindergarten through college. There was simply no way I could remember the names of all my teachers. What WAS my kindergarten teacher's name, anyway?

They also inquired as to every place I had ever lived and every foreign country I'd ever visited, including exact dates of these visits. Now my mother was English, having met my father during WWII while he was stationed in England. I had gone to England with her a few times when I was very young to visit my relatives there. I had no idea as to the exact dates of these visits. Quite a few of the other questions on these forms were just as impossible for me to answer.

There were also questions about any crimes I may have committed as well as sticky questions regarding drug use. I was as meticulously honest as I could be regarding my marijuana smoking. Luckily I had no other crimes to report.

On and on it went. When they first mentioned not returning for an hour I thought I would have lots of time to kill before they returned. As it turned out, I had barely finished with the forms when I heard the door open behind me. My coffee stood stone cold on the desk beside me. I literally hadn't had a single moment to drink it.

Bill asked: "Have you completed all the forms?"

"Yes, but I have some questions about some of them. For example, there is no way I can remember all of my teachers' names."

Bill said sympathetically: "No problem, as long as you have honestly filled out all that you are able to, that will be fine."

John held out his hand and said: "Thank you for coming, Mr. Connor. We will evaluate the information you have provided us and will get back to you shortly. It's been a pleasure to meet you and I hope you have a good day."

I said: "That's it? Aren't you going to tell me any more about the job?"

"Not at the present time," John replied. "We will go over your material and if we think we still have an opportunity for you we will be in contact. Again, it was a pleasure to meet you and I wish you a good day."

Well, that was all a big waste of time! What the hell was going on? Had they just brought me downtown to jerk me around? For this, I got my haircut? What a joke!

After that short visit to Wonderland, I returned to my normal life of schoolwork and socializing with friends. I got through my last month of school without any word from Bill or John. I asked Dr. Bazhenov if he knew anything about the results of my interview, but he said he had no idea of how it went and that I should just be patient.

I graduated with my degree in Political Science in mid-June and reported that fact to my draft board, as required by law. Summer loomed before me and I was completely unsure what to do. It seemed a waste of time to search for a law school as I was surely going to be drafted very soon. A few weeks after I graduated a new draft card appeared in the mail for me. It now showed my status as I-A, which meant I was prime meat for the draft. Should I enlist in the Coast Guard? Some of my friends were doing so, but at this point even the Coast Guard was getting involved in the Vietnam War.

Then finally, a letter came postmarked from the Presidio. At that time, the

Presidio was still a small, but active, Army base at the northern tip of San Francisco. It was famous (or notorious) as the location where the order was signed to send all Japanese-Americans, including citizens, to internment camps during the Second World War. It had more wooded areas than built-up areas and thus looked more like a park than a military facility. Lots of anti-war demonstrations had taken place at its gates during that year.

My stomach sank, and I very reluctantly tore open the envelope. Was this an induction notice? The letter inside was typed, but with no letterhead or even any signature. It simply requested that I come to the Building 14A, Room 201, in the Presidio of San Francisco on Friday at 10:00 AM for a continuation of my mid-May interview. It also stated that I should be prepared to spend the entire day at the Presidio. There was a telephone number to call if I was unable to make the appointment. What the heck was going on? I guess I would find out on Friday.

I made sure to arrive an hour early for my appointment because I didn't want to be delayed trying to find Building 14A. I asked directions at the base gate and an MP actually offered to lead me there. I thought that a bit strange, but I followed his jeep to the building and was soon in the lobby. Although early, I walked to Room 201 and found its door locked. So, I returned to the lobby and waited for the appointed hour. I uncomfortably stared at recruiting posters on the walls. None of them featured pictures of Vietnam. One even showed smiling soldiers standing in front of the Coliseum in Rome, with their beautiful Italian girlfriends looking up adoringly at them. All of them made Army life look like a continuous vacation.

At exactly 3 minutes before 10:00 AM, I started walking back to Room 201 and found to my great relief that this time the door opened into a small office. Sitting at the desk was John, looking car salesman-like as ever. All he needed was a large checked sports coat to complete the look.

Upon my entry, he immediately arose from his chair, stretched out his hand, and warmly greeted me.

"Good morning, Mr. Connor. I hope all is well with you." He glanced down at a paper on his desk and said: "I see you have graduated with honors. Congratulations!"

I thanked him. He gestured for me to sit down in the chair in front of his desk. He reached into a desk drawer and pulled out a very fat manila folder, placed it on the desk before him, and proceeded to leaf through its contents. He then raised his head and said, "Before we continue any further - I see that you have used some recreational marijuana during your college days. This seems to be more and more the norm today, but I must inform you that for us to continue any further in this process you must commit to immediately stop any and all illegal drug use. You must firmly vow to us that you will never use any of these substances again as long as you are associated with us. If you do so affirm, and at some point in the future you fail to comply with your promise, I assure you that you will suffer the direst consequences, up to and including prosecution and imprisonment. Do I make myself clear on this point?"

"Absolutely," I said, and I meant it!

"Do you now affirm to immediately cease all use of illegal drugs of any kind?"

"I do."

"Mr. Connor I think we are now ready to make you a job offer. I assume you are still interested in the position we discussed with you?"

I said: "You really never told me what the position is, but yes, I'm still interested based on the little I actually know about it."

John laughed, and said: "Fair enough. Please let me fill you in on what we have in mind for you." And so he did.

3

NSA – THE GREAT PUZZLE PALACE

John then said: "Have you ever heard of an organization called the National Security Agency?"

I replied: "No, I haven't."

John went on in his usual formal way: "It was officially established on November 4, 1952. I'm not surprised that you've never heard of it, its very existence has been kept quite secret up until very recently. For many years its employees have joked that NSA really stood for No Such Agency."

I laughed politely at what I thought was a pretty lame joke.

"The NSA's core mission is to protect our nation's secure communications and to produce foreign signals intelligence. In brief, we make codes for the US and listen in on the communications of other nations and break their codes. This is the organization I work for and the organization where we would like to see you working."

I was totally surprised. Code making and code breaking? I could see that my math background might conceivably be useful for doing that, but I really knew nothing about cryptography. Why did they seem so interested in my odd academic background? What possible job could I do for them?

I told John of my concerns. He said, "What we have in mind for you is a very unique opportunity. It will certainly utilize your background in math and languages and will involve you using a computer to perform your job. We are more than willing to provide you with all of the training you may require in the use of computers. The bottom line is this job will involve attempting to accomplish something that has never been done before, but a task we think can be accomplished by a team of talented professionals; a team in which we feel you can play an important role. It should be exciting and extremely challenging work and it is work that will provide a very powerful new capability for helping protect and defend our country from its enemies. The work will be performed at Fort Meade, Maryland, where the NSA headquarters is located. That's right between Baltimore, Maryland and Washington, DC. I cannot overstate how important this project is to the NSA and our nation. This is really all I can tell you about the project right now, but I hope it has been enough to convince you to seriously consider joining our team. Are you interested?"

I was completely flabbergasted by what he said. What possible talent could I bring to such a mysterious team? A team working on something vitally important to our nation? Again – why me?

I said: "I'm really surprised by everything you've just told me. Can I take some time to decide what to do?"

John replied: "Certainly you can take some time. I know how difficult it must be for you to make such a big decision based on such little knowledge, but I think if you give it some serious consideration you'll come to the correct decision. Please remember that you cannot discuss this opportunity, or anything I told you about our organization or its work, with anyone. Not your family, not your friends, your pastor, no one. This is a decision you'll need to make all by yourself. I do feel confident that in the end you will decide to take up this challenge and serve your country. Nevertheless, whatever you decide, I want to wish you the greatest success in your life. I think you are an especially talented individual."

I thanked him for his kind words to me, but he wasn't finished.

"One thing – if you can make your decision immediately, we are willing to start the hiring process right here, right now. We have a team here at the Presidio that's ready to assist you in the process of joining the NSA. There will be some paperwork that will need to be filled out and processed, some further interviews, and some security procedures that need to be accomplished. So, would you be ready to give us an answer right now? It would certainly expedite the hiring process and would also protect you immediately from being subjected to the draft. I imagine that must be a concern of yours. In fact, you may very well receive an induction notice any day now."

Decide immediately? Was this a veiled threat that I might be immediately drafted if I didn't say yes? Or was I just being paranoid? Why shouldn't I just decide now? I certainly wasn't going to be able to discuss this with anyone else, what with all the secrecy surrounding it. Why not just say yes? What were the downsides, if any, to doing so? On the other hand, why the big rush?

I said: "Can I just take a few minutes to collect my thoughts before giving you an answer?"

"Of course you can. Why don't you just go back to the lobby, think it over for a while, and then return here when you've made a decision? I'll be here for the next hour or so and will await your decision."

An hour or so? Was that going to be enough time? What if I said I needed still more time? Would this opportunity vanish? Would I end up in Vietnam? What the hell should I do?

I got up from my chair, exited the office, and walked back to the lobby. By the time I reached the lobby I realized that I had really already made my decision. So, I turned right around and walked right back to John's office. This time I knocked, and he said: "Come in."

"I've decided to join the NSA."

"Excellent, I'm so happy to hear that from you. I think you've made the right decision and I'm sure you are going to find this to be a real positive turning point in your life. Congratulations!" With that John gave me a hearty handshake and vigorous pat on my back. He actually appeared to be very happy with what I'd just decided. The truth is that he was under huge pressure to get all the staff on board that would be needed to start up the project he had mentioned to me. That was what was behind the rush to get me signed up with the NSA. I was just one of many people he was now chasing after.

"Come with me and I'll guide you through the process of entering employment with the Agency." I did just that.

I won't bore the reader with all of the bureaucratic mumbo-jumbo I endured for the rest of the day at the Presidio except to talk about the most surprising part of the whole entry into the world of the NSA: the lie-detector test. I was completely shocked to be subjected to one. I had only seen lie detectors on TV and in the movies, and then only used to interrogate criminals. Why were they giving one to me?

The examiner who operated the machine and asked me questions was named Ralph. Ralph was a short balding man wearing slacks, a white shirt open at the collar, and a gray vest. He looked pretty disheveled and he seemed to sweat even more than I did during this very stressful experience. The test proceeded very much like in the movies with Ralph at first asking very innocuous questions. He said that was to establish a baseline of my physiological responses. These registered on the paper strip coming out of the machine. All during the test I heard the scratch, scratch, scratch of the pens on the paper strip, sounding like ten cats scratching to get into a house.

What really amazed me was how long the test went on (over 2 hours) and how bizarre some of the questions were. Of course Ralph spent quite a bit of time on my drug use, asking what seemed to be the exact same questions over and over again regarding every aspect of my dope smoking. After that he started up on my sex life.

"Do you ever find yourself sexually aroused by small children?"
"Have you ever had a sexual encounter with an animal?"
"Have you ever had sex with a close relative?"

...And so on. I was asked questions about sexual activities that I honestly had never even imagined as being possible. Weird stuff, indeed!

The lie-detector ordeal closed with lots of questions about my political beliefs and whether I had any type of contact with anyone I believed to be a Communist or with anyone who was a sympathizer with Communist ideology. When the testing was finally over, I felt physically and emotionally drained. Little did I realize that this would not be the last time I would endure a lie-detector test during my career within the intelligence community. I would actually have to take one every 3 to 5 years. I was just happy to be done with this deeply disturbing experience. Future tests would gradually become easier to bear, but never be enjoyable.

I finally got into my car well after 7:00 PM that day, and drove home completely exhausted. I left the Presidio with a binder filled with information that John felt was important for me to have. In it was a sheet of paper with a phone number I was to immediately call if I received a draft notice. Another sheet of paper contained the phone number of a moving company to call for arranging my move to Maryland. I had color brochures on life in Anne Arundel County, the "land of pleasant living". It was the county in which Fort Meade was located. I also had cheery brochures on Howard County and Prince George's County, both adjacent counties to Anne Arundel. Apparently, both of these had plenty of available apartments. I had information on an account that had been set up for me in the NSA Credit Union. I had page after page on security regulations – which basically told me to assume that every stranger I met was a Soviet agent. What had I just signed up for? Had I made a huge mistake? I was actually shocked at what I had just done. It really seemed a pretty rash decision to make so hastily.

Well, after I got home to my pad in Height-Asbury, I just became resigned to my new life in government service. It wasn't law school, but I also wasn't going to end up in Vietnam, either. Maybe law school might still be in my future when and if the blasted war ever ended. Then I could just thumb my nose at the NSA, quit, apply to a law school, and have enough money saved in the bank to get me all the way through school.

Of course, I couldn't tell anyone where I was really going to be working. I had been briefed to tell my friends and family that I had just taken a job with "the Federal government". If pressed for further details, I was to say that I was employed within "the Department of Defense". I was to deflect further questioning whenever possible, and if necessary state that I was "working in a clerical position". Any further pressing beyond that level of detail and I was to immediately call the Security Department for further guidance. I had yet another phone number for them. I also had the feeling that if I actually had to call the Security Department that whoever was asking me questions was about to end up having a very bad day.

The next two weeks were a whirl of activity arranging my move across country, saying goodbyes to family and friends, and constantly second-guessing the decision I had just made. I was only twenty two years old and even the smallest thing seemed a huge deal to me at that point in my life. So, making this decision seemed like a truly gigantic thing to me. I was constantly wondering if I hadn't ruined my life by my hasty decision. If I had been drafted, maybe I would have ended up stationed in Germany, or even in the US. Had I been a complete idiot?

Anyway, moving day came and I had to admit the NSA knew how to organize a cross-county move. The moving company took care of absolutely everything. Packers came the day before the move and boxed up all of my rather meager processions. When I wasn't watching them they even packed my trashcan, complete with trash. The next day a moving van appeared at my door and a crew of men loaded up the boxes and the few pieces of furniture I hadn't given away to my struggling fellow students.

Then it was off in my car for the cross-country drive. I was to accomplish the drive in 5 days, finally arriving at the Holiday Inn in Laurel, Maryland – my temporary home until I found an apartment. My reservation there had been made and prepaid by the NSA.

I called another one of the vast set of phone numbers in my binder to report my arrival and was told to spend the next few days looking for housing. I actually found an apartment the very next day in Laurel only about 15 minutes away from Fort Meade. The NSA Housing Assistance Department made all difficulties in getting my lease signed and approved quickly disappear. Of course, their phone number was also in my binder.

4

STARTING MY NEW JOB

After calling the Personnel Department (you know where their phone number was to be found) and reporting that I had located an apartment and given them my address, after a short time on hold I was told to report to work the next day. I was to be prepared to show my driver's license at the guard gate and I would receive a temporary parking pass for my car and be told where to park. I was to report to the Headquarters Building and ask to be directed to the Personnel Department.

The Headquarters Building was only five years old at that time and it looked absolutely gigantic to me. It was said that the US Capitol could fit inside it four times with room to spare. This building was reputed to have the longest uninterrupted hallway in the world. It had darkened one-way glass and looked like a gigantic elongated black cube. The NSA was actually the largest single employer in the State of Maryland at that time. For all I know, it still may be.

I parked my car, placed the temporary parking pass the guard gave me on the dashboard, and hiked to the lobby of the giant monolith. I walked up to the large counter in the middle of the lobby, gave them my driver's license, and told them I was a new employee reporting for work. I asked to be directed to the Personnel Office. The security officer at the desk very nonchalantly called Personnel, squinted at my license, and gave them my name. They must have vouchsafed me, because he hung up the phone and gave me my license back and handed me a red-colored temporary badge.

He said mechanically: "Be sure to wear the badge at all times. Step through the turnstile to my left, and go down that hall until you come to a large double door on the right with 'Personnel' it. Then go right in, they are expecting you."

With that he pressed a button on his desk to release the lock on the turnstile and I did as he said. It was quite a long walk down the hall to my destination.

I entered into the Personnel Office and came up to another counter. I again identified myself and was quickly escorted to a small windowless room. There, believe it or not, I had even more paperwork to review and sign. I had my picture taken and was given a red and white laminated photo ID badge that did not have even the slightest hint on it that I actually worked for the NSA. All it said was DOD.

I was then informed that I had actually just been granted Conditional Employment at this point, contingent upon my passing a background investigation and completing the security clearance process. Conditional Employment! Oh crap, all of my fears about my decision returned with a vengeance. I must have turned pale when I was told this, because the nice personnel lady I was dealing with immediately reassured me that she was sure I would pass all these hurdles with flying colors.

Next, I was sent off for psychological testing, which involved filling out more questionnaires followed by an hour-long interview with a psychologist. Eventually I was sent home for the day. I did have an appointment the next morning with a Mr. Withers at 11:00 AM on the 3rd floor of the Headquarters Building. I was told that he would be able to get me actually started in doing some real work for the NSA.

The next day I showed up early, as usual, for my appointment with Mr. Withers. I was ushered into his office and found him to be a gray-haired man with crew cut, white shirt, black tie, gray slacks, and a huge grin. He had a positively booming voice, a strong Southern accent, and he asked how I was getting along so far.

"I'm doing fine, but I still have no idea what I'm going to be doing here."

Withers replied: "Ah, yes…well…let me see if I can't straighten things out for you a little. What you're going to be doing right now is going to a training school. It looks to me like you will be attending IBM training for the next six months. The classes are held in IBM's facility just down the road from here. You're going to be taking just about every class they offer from Introduction to Data Processing all the way up to Advanced Assembly Language Programming. We've got you booked solid…I think you may have one two-week period without any classes, but we've tried to be very efficient in making the absolute best use of your time. By the time you have completed this training you should be an absolute computer wizard. You should also have completed the entire security clearance process and be ready to hit the ground running with your project. Yes, you'll be raring to go after all that training."

"And what is the project I'll be working on? What will be the most important things for me to learn during my training?"

"Well, I really can't get into that right now. Not until you have completed the security clearance process. So, I'd have to say...learn all you can about programming computers!"

Just great, I thought to myself. I'm to learn everything I can so that I can do my best possible work on a mystery project that I know nothing about. What a mad house!

Of course what I actually said was: "Great, I'm looking forward to learning all I can about computers. Where do I go and when do I start?"

The next Monday found me at the nearby IBM facility. IBM had built a giant office building just to service the computing needs of the NSA. The NSA was probably IBM's biggest single customer at this point in time and IBM pulled out all the stops in providing whatever the NSA needed. Their facility was modern, roomy, and quite impressive looking. It featured an architecture of lots of chrome and steel with dark tinted windows.

The first floor housed a huge data center that contained one or more examples of virtually every single mainframe computer system that IBM manufactured at that time. There were also keypunch machines, verifiers (machines used to manually verify that punch cards had been created correctly), card sorters, card collators, high-speed parallel printers, and electronic accounting machines (plug-board wired precursors to digital computer that were still in limited use at that time). This was the age in which the 80-column IBM card still ruled supreme. Personal computers were over 10 years away. Computer terminals were rare, expensive, and exotic devices. The only mice around were unwanted rodents that would quickly be exterminated if found. The noise level within the data center was substantial with card readers clattering, printers hammering, and a constant whir from the hundreds of fans that were required for keeping these giant electronic brains properly cooled. I immediately loved all of it - it was so awesome!

The floors above the data center contained sales offices, support offices, and a complete training center with dozens of classrooms. The classrooms were filled with modern office chairs, tables, screens and slide projectors. Only one of them had any computer terminals in it. Down the hall from the classroom was a keypunch room with machines available for the use of the students. Yes, we were expected to actually type our programs onto IBM cards.

In the olden days of sailing ships there was a commonly used term describing the experience of the sailors at that time – "wooden ships and iron men". Today we can look back at this point in the history of computers and just might say that there were "wooden computers and iron programmers".

This was because programming these giant, slow beasts was truly an extremely painful process. Programs were handwritten onto source programming forms and then had to be keypunched onto IBM cards, either by the programmer themselves or by a "keypunch girl". There were armies of keypunch girls employed at this time for inputting data into mainframe computers. Often times after being keypunched, the card decks were passed onto verifiers. These women sat at a verifier machine and completely retyped the entire program again. The verifier looked just like a keypunch machine, but it actually just read already keypunched cards and compared their contents to the keyboard input from the person retyping the data. If a keystroke did not match the actual contents of the punched card, the keyboard would lock. At that point the verifier operator would manually inspect the card (yes, you could learn to actually read the contents of the cards from the pattern of holes in them), and either re-punch the entire card or just patch the incorrect column in the card with a tiny adhesive sticker and then only re-punch the errant column.

When the keypunching of a program was finally completed, its set of IBM cards was next put into a long tray and taken to the input window of the computer center. Eventually the tray would be passed onto a computer operator who would get it into the mainframe via a punch card reader. This reader could read punch cards at a whopping 1000 cards per minute. Then the program went into an electronic "job queue" for eventual execution. Depending upon the priority assigned to this particular job, it might take quite some time before it was actually executed on the mainframe.

Eventually the source program would be compiled by the computer - that is translated into actual machine language, and a listing would be produced showing any errors the program contained. The source program tray and its associated program listing would then slowly make its way onto an output shelf. The programmer would regularly check his own particular shelf and would eventually be able to retrieve the deck and the listing. He would then tear his hair out over any mistakes he had made, as clearly shown by the compilation listing error messages. He would next correct the mistakes and resubmit the corrected deck at the input window. If lucky, he might get three or four compilations a day, and these were just compilations that were needed to catch all of the syntax errors in the source code, not even an actual execution of the program itself. As you can imagine, software development in those days was an excruciating and extraordinarily time-consuming activity. Hence, "wooden computers and iron programmers"!

I learned all of this at the IBM training center. Since it was all that was really possible at the time it all seemed quite normal to me and actually pretty amazing. I had all of this computing power at my beck and call, if somewhat slowly and erratically. I discovered that I loved playing with computers! I still didn't know what I was going to use them for but I was now sure it would be a whole lot of fun for me to write computer programs.

The six months of training fairly flew by, and low and behold I now possessed yet another binder – this one full of certificates of completion for all of the IBM training courses I had attended. IBM training was normally very expensive, but I have a feeling given the hundreds of millions of dollars that the NSA was spending on their hardware, that IBM was more than happy to provide it all to me completely free of charge.

Coincident with my completing training, I was informed that all of the background investigations and security clearance processes had been completed and that I had been granted a TS/SCI clearance. That stood for Top Secret/Sensitive Compartmentalized Information and was one of the very highest clearance levels possible from the Department of Defense. I breathed a huge sigh of relief at that news. So, I was finally going to learn exactly what the NSA wanted me to do for them.

In early February of 1969 I reported to the Personnel Office in the Headquarters building again. I brought along my binder full of IBM training certificates just in case they wanted to verify that I had actually completed all of my scheduled courses. It wasn't necessary, but with all the bureaucracy I had been dealing with so far, it wouldn't have surprised me to be challenged to prove that I had actually attended the training and hadn't just spent the entire time goofing off.

After a half hour wait, I was ushered into the office of Mrs. Perkins. She looked very prim and proper in a dark blue dress and eyeglasses that were perched on the end of her nose.

Guess what – she wanted me to sign more forms! I did as instructed. She asked for my badge, which I handed to her. She took a new picture of me and shortly afterward handed me a new laminated photo ID badge. This differed from my old badge in that it was blue and white and contained a transparent thin green stripe diagonally across its front.

Mrs. Perkins then said: "Congratulations, Mr. Connor. You have now passed from Conditional Employment to Full Employment with the Technology Directorate of the Agency." Mrs. Perkins then instructed me to report up to Mr. Withers' third floor office again – the very same office I had been in over 6 months ago. Off I went.

Upon arriving there Mr. Withers said to me: "Well, congratulations Mr. Connor." It was turning into a day filled with congratulating people.

"We've been receiving excellent reports from IBM on your progress through their training program. You were actually one of their top students. I think if we didn't already employ you that IBM might actually have made you a job offer. In any case, you are now ready to join our team. We will be meeting in Room 4007 at 1:00 PM today. We will be introducing you to the team and discussing the project's progress up to now. You'll meet the other team members and start learning about the expectations we have for your participation in the project. In the meantime, I'll show you to your cubicle. It's also on the 4th floor."

"Wait a minute," I said. "Can't you tell me what the project is all about? I have no idea what will be discussed during this afternoon's meeting. I think I'll feel like a complete idiot if I continue to have absolutely no idea what this project is trying to accomplish."

"Oh, I'm sorry, of course how foolish of me. Let me give you a brief explanation of Project Litany".

5

MY SCIENCE FICTION PROJECT FINALLY REVEALED

He then said to me: "We are going to create an automated system to translate Russian documents into English. Nothing like this has ever been tried before, but we are convinced that we finally have the expertise and the technology available to accomplish this. It's going to be a real challenge, but the payoff will be huge. The NSA is drowning in Russian documents and we can't hire enough translators to keep up with the load. In addition, the quality of translations we get varies tremendously and we are constantly having heated arguments between translators about subtle differences in the precise meaning of documents. A huge advantage of having the entire process automated is that we will have consistent and predictable translations performed on every document. Only a few special cases will need to be handled manually for dealing with some of the peculiar nuisances of the Russian language."

I swear, my jaw dropped at this news. This was absolutely science fiction. Using computers to translate Russian to English. It seemed like an impossible task!

Now I know what you, dear reader, are thinking. What's the big deal? Google Translate will quite easily do this very thing right now on my cell phone. Please remember, this was 1969 and the biggest, baddest, supercomputers available at that time were toys compared to the computing power you now carry in your pocket. It was truly almost unimaginable to even consider accomplishing such a task with the primitive computers then available. So, please be patient with the Project Litany team and try and understand just how monumental this task appeared to us all at the time. I frankly doubted if it could even be done when I first heard of it. After all of my training I was painfully aware of just how difficult such a task would be to accomplish with the computers then available to us.

If you were ever a fan of the original Star Trek television series, you'll likely remember this famous quote of Spock's: "I am endeavoring, ma'am, to construct a mnemonic memory circuit using stone knives and bearskins." To me, this quote catches the essence of the task the Project Litany team had been given to accomplish.

After Bob (I finally found out Mr. Withers' first name) showed me my cubicle, I basically just killed time until the afternoon status meeting. I found out where the nearest water fountains were, where the nearest men's room was located, where the cafeteria was to be found, and what kinds of meals they offered for lunch. Finally, Bob Withers dropped by my cube and led me into Room 4007 for the Project Litany status meeting.

I was wondering why the project was called "Litany". I later found out that it was the practice of the NSA to pick random names for all of their projects. The names had nothing to do with the purpose of the project, which I think was exactly the reason for picking them randomly. If some Soviet agent learned of a project name, he would have no idea what the project actually entailed.

Meeting Room 4007 had a very long highly polished wooden table located in its center. A large screen hung at the end of the room opposite the entrance and a slide projector sat at the other end on the table. Swivel chairs lined both sides of the table and more lined the sidewalls. All of the windows were covered with thick drapes. It looked like the room would be able to hold about 25 people around the table, and at least that many more in the chairs along the walls.

People soon started filing into the meeting room. What I saw was primarily a whole bunch of crew cuts and white shirts. Bob and I sat at the middle of the table and Bob greeted each team member as they entered. As soon as Bob said one team member's name, I forgot the previous name. I simply have a terrible memory for people's names. This went on until the last team member entered the room. At that point there were about 30 of us in there. Bob asked someone to close the door and he stood and walked to the far end of the table.

"Good afternoon, everyone. The first order of business today is to introduce a new member of our team. Mr. Connor, please stand." I did as instructed.

"Everyone, this is Stephen Connor. Mr. Connor has joined us as a programmer on the team. Would everyone please take a brief moment to introduce yourself to Stephen, giving your name and your role in the project? Let's start with you, Michael."

"My name is Michael Henderson, and I'm an electrical engineer on the team."

"I'm Jack Smithers, mechanical engineering."

"I'm Ralph Thompson, linguist."

"I'm Maria Jacobson, linguist."

"George Harris, programmer." George then nodded to me in a brief acknowledgment of our common role in the team.

"Reggie Smith, optics."

"Roger Clooney, systems analyst."

"Harold Gordon, mechanical engineer."

And on and on it went. It turned out that we had twenty-eight people on the Project Litany team. 1-project manager, 2-linguists, 5-electrical engineers, 2-optical engineers, 5-mechanical engineers, 12-programmers including myself, and 1-systems analyst. This was the team that had set out to accomplish the near impossible. Little did anyone realize it at the time, but it would take us 4 years to finish this task.

I won't bore you with all of the technical details on exactly how we accomplished this task. After all, you started reading this story because you wanted to hear about spies, not programming and engineering problems. I've only taken you down this path so far because it's the path that led me to my final field operational roles – much more exciting stuff. So, for now, please just try and be patient.

On December of 1972, the draft was officially ended. So, if I were really serious about ever quitting the NSA and entering law school there was now nothing holding me back from doing exactly that. After only the very briefest consideration of this option, I immediately discarded that idea. I simply loved playing with computers, and the NSA was the perfect spot to work for people like me. On top of that, Project Litany seemed to finally be reaching completion and I definitely wanted to be around to see it actually go into operation. I had spent far too many years slaving away on this project to walk away from it when it was so near to becoming a reality.

So, on March of 1973 we were finally able to demonstrate our prototype system to the top brass of the NSA. Not only had we come up with a software solution for producing reasonable translations of technical Russian into English, but we had also managed to build the first practical working Optical Character

Recognition (OCR) readers. Our OCR readers could read pages of Russian documents and the Cyrillic characters contained in them would be digitally captured. The entire page image was also digitized into a graphical format so that any drawings or diagrams contained in it could also be reproduced.

Next the digitized Cyrillic characters would be transferred onto the hard disk drives of our IBM System/360 Model 95. This was the largest supercomputer that IBM made at the time. It could perform a whopping 330 million multiplications per minute. The laptop I am using today to write this book can perform about 10 billion multiplications per SECOND, so you can see how slow this behemoth actually was compared to today's computers.

Not only were we limited in computing power; the memory limitations of the system were equally severe. Our System/360 Model 95 had the absolute maximum amount of memory possible installed on it, and this consisted of 4 megabytes of fairly slow core RAM memory, and 16 megabytes of faster solid state RAM memory. Again, the laptop on which I'm writing this book has 4 gigabytes of solid state RAM, memory inconceivably faster than that of the Model 95, and 200 times more of it.

We also had to cope with additional problems because of disk space limitations, but I think you get the idea. So, the programs we managed to write to perform the translation task had to use every trick we could come up with in order to perform the process in a reasonable amount of time and work within all the hardware limitations we had. Almost all of the programs we created were written in Assembly Language, which was just a slightly shorthand version of the actual internal machine language of the computer. It was the hardest programming language to master, but it was absolutely the most efficient in utilizing the limited memory and processing power we then had available to us. We literally had to write over a half million lines of Assembly Language code to accomplish this task and the hours that were required to write, compile, and test this code were monumental. Every team member worked astonishing overtime hours to get the job done.

The bottom line was that when we finally finished it all worked amazingly well. Documents went into the OCR readers and in a few minutes a high-speed printer attached to our Model 95 printed out a reasonably accurate English translation of the document. We also had plotters attached to the computer that could reproduce images of the original document in order to display any drawings or diagrams contained in it, if need be. The damn thing actually worked!

Applause and accolades were showered on the entire team. Every one of us ended up getting a promotion and some type of award from the NSA. I was promoted to Senior Programmer. We had taken a huge step in breaking the bottleneck of untranslated Russian documents that the NSA had acquired. Soon our OCR readers were digesting documents by the bushel and our printers spitting out translations by the mile. We were absolute heroes within the NSA world and everyone loved us. Life was wonderful!

6

ONWARD, UPWARD, AND OUTWARD

All the team members were given their choice of new assignments. We were the whiz kids and everyone in the Technology Directorate wanted us. I entertained a plethora of offers and finally chose one that I thought would be especially interesting. It was to create an automated intelligence analyst workstation.

CRT terminals were now finally becoming more commonly available and more reasonably priced. The Internet was also just beginning to come into existence. Its first appearance was in the form of the Department of Defense ARPAnet network. A couple of dozen computers were already attached to this network and we were just starting to figure out how powerful such networking capabilities could be. Minicomputers were also coming onto the scene, greatly reducing the cost of computing. The UNIX operating system was escaping from Bell Labs and onto minicomputers around the world. Relational database software was starting to become available, finally enabling large amounts of information to be stored on disk drives and organized in a systematic manner for quick and easy retrieval.

Mainframes also continued to get bigger. IBM's System/360 line of computers was being replaced by the new System/370 line, which featured larger capacity disk drives, more RAM, and faster processors. In fact, Project Litany was in the process of being moved onto a System/370 Model 168 from our now old and decrepit System/360 Model 95. How quickly the mighty fall in the computer world!

What the NSA wanted now was a standardized workstation for their intelligence analysts to use for evaluating what was known within the Agency as

SIGINT. This is simply eavesdropping on the electronic emissions produced by foreign nations. SIGINT was further divided into COMINT: the interception of communications signals, ELINT: the gathering of information on radar, radar jammers, and other similar electronic devices, and TELINT: the gathering of telemetry data transmitted by automatic devices contained in aircraft, missiles, or spacecraft. A new generation of spy satellites was going to be launched in the upcoming years that would be capable of providing the NSA with a gigantic amount of such data. The intelligence analysts who needed to sift through it all would require some kind of advanced computer workstations to aid them in organizing and deciphering this information. I was to work on the software required to make these specialized workstations do their jobs. It was going to be a lot of fun!

Much of the software that I wrote for this workstation was pretty arcane, so I'm not going to go into a lot of detail regarding what it did or how it worked. I will say that the entire software development process had made a huge leap forward since my work started on Project Litany. We now had dedicated software development workstations with CRT terminals and had escaped the world of punch cards entirely. We could create software right on our own terminals and then submit the source code immediately for compilation on a dedicated minicomputer. We then got immediate feedback on any errors our code contained. Thus the entire software development cycle was drastically shortened and made infinitely easier for we poor programmers. We were also becoming a lot savvier about the best way to design software in a modular manner. In addition, we devoted much more time to the high-level architecture of the system before we went off and started writing code. All of this made our software easier to test and update and reduced the need to work phenomenally long hours getting our software up and running.

I was responsible for most of the design of the workstation software and wrote a fair portion of the code myself. I also came up with some fairly innovative supporting software that greatly aided in testing the correct functionality of our code. I was really hitting my stride as a software developer.

So, instead of four years, we were able to complete this project in only one year. In April 1974 prototypes of our new workstations were put into use by a few dozen selected intelligence analysts and these proved to be extremely successful. The intelligence analysts loved them, and so did their bosses, and most importantly, our bosses and their bosses. Again, I found myself characterized as a super whiz kid programmer. I actually was turning into a pretty good software developer and could easily see myself moving into a team leader role, or even a new role that was just starting to appear in the software world: a software architect. This lofty position involved creating development standards, high-level designs, and design templates that all of the programmers needed to follow. What a wonderful job that would be!

Then a totally unexpected thing happened. I mentioned before just how poorly the CIA and NSA got along with each other. It seemed like they were rivals in everything. If the CIA got a nifty new supercomputer, the NSA immediately ordered two of them. The NSA was definitely a military environment while the CIA was all Ivy League. Cats and dogs got along better than they did.

However, unbeknownst to most of the lowly employees of these organizations, the big bosses from each of these agencies sometimes met and chatted about possibly mutually beneficial activities. They didn't like each other, but they sometimes needed each other. Apparently during one of these conversations the topic of the NSA's nifty new intelligence analyst workstation came up. I'm sure it all started with someone from the NSA bragging about their technological superiority over the CIA, but it eventually turned into a more serious discussion – one something like baseball team owners often have. Some type of trade talks then started. Something along the lines of "I'll trade you this shortstop for that pitcher." The talks between these agencies somehow progressed into "I'll transfer some special funding we have received from Congress to you for the programmer that designed your workstation software." I had been traded to a new team, and like most ballplayers I had no idea about what was being planned until it actually happened to me.

A few weeks later I was called all the way up to the 9th floor of the headquarters building and into the office of a very senior manager at the NSA. I believe he was a Navy Admiral and he certainly looked the part. He had gray hair and a really weather-beaten face that he, no doubt, got from many days standing on the bridge of his flagship barking out orders to the crew.

He said: "Mr. Connor, I would like to again congratulate you on the very fine work you have accomplished on both our language translation system and the new analyst workstation."

I thanked him with as humble a pose as I could muster, actually veritably bursting with pride at receiving a compliment from such a lofty personage.

"We are wondering if you might like to take on something of a special project. It would involve helping our sister agency, the CIA, in creating a similar workstation for their intelligence analysts in Langley. It would be a huge help to them, and of course, to your country. What do think about that?"

Our "sister agency"? That was the first time I had heard the CIA described that way by anyone in the NSA. I should have immediately realized that something seriously unusual was up, but I continued to just be smug about what a whiz kid I had become.

"Of course I would be more that happy to help our sister agency," I replied with pride.

"Wonderful, I'm really happy to see that you are so enthusiastic about this project. I'd like you to head downstairs to Personnel and ask to see a Mr. Fleming. Again, I want to personally thank and congratulate you on your outstanding work here. You did an amazing job and I want you to know how much it has been appreciated." With that he stood, shook my hand, and effectively dismissed me by sitting back down, picking up some papers on his desk, and starting to read them. It was like I was suddenly invisible to him.

Now, I may have been naive, but I wasn't a complete idiot. Why was I going to Personnel? Nothing good ever came from being sent to the Personnel Office. Why had it felt like my accomplishments had just been discussed in the past tense? How could I feel praised and also feel like I was about to be fired at the very same time? The NSA was sometimes a strange place to work, but all of this was exceptionally bizarre.

So, I left his office and took the elevator down to Personnel. There I asked for Mr. Fleming.

Mr. Fleming turned out to be very unlike most of the NSA employees I had been working with so far. The NSA was definitely part of the Department of Defense and it was primarily populated by active duty or retired military. The Director was always a very senior military officer, and the Directorship rotated through all the branches of the armed services. At that time we had an Army General as our Director.

Mr. Fleming looked totally out of place. Instead of the crew cut, white shirt, and black skinny tie that seemed to be the uniform here for men, his jet black wavy hair was unusually long and he wore a three-piece corduroy suit with a dark blue shirt and wide paisley tie. The paisley tie was the first I'd seen since I had left San Francisco.

When Mr. Fleming spoke it was with a Boston accent: "Good afternoon, Mr. Connor. It's really good to finally meet you. I've heard so much about you and what an absolute genius you are at designing software. How are you, today?"

"A little confused. Just why have I been sent down to Personnel?"

"Why, to arrange for your transfer to the Central Intelligence Agency. You mean this hasn't been discussed with you?"

"No, it hasn't."

"Oh my goodness, no wonder you seem confused. I find it hard to believe that you would be sent to speak with me without extensive prior discussions about your transfer. I had assumed you had been involved in lengthy talks about it and had fully agreed that it would be most beneficial for your career in government service to make this transfer. I'm positively speechless that you seem so surprised by all of this. Absolutely shocked!" He lied wonderfully well. Many years later I found out that this whole charade had been arranged between the NSA and CIA to squeeze me into quick compliance with the transfer. There had never been any intention on either party's part to consult with me regarding this player trade between the two teams. Why would they bother?

"Well, tell me what it's all about, then," I said, completely deflated from my previous prideful state. I was finally figuring out that I was not an irreplaceable whiz kid, after all, and felt more like a lamb being led to slaughter.

Mr. Fleming said: "Well, this is really a wonderful opportunity for you. You are being promoted to a Lead Programmer position and will be working on a vitally important software development project for the CIA. Your expertise is sorely needed there and I know that you were specifically selected for this very important role. People at the CIA are already talking about you and the extraordinary talents you will be bringing to The Company (a nickname of the CIA at that time). Your fellow team members are thrilled at the prospect of working with you. We all consider ourselves very fortunate, indeed, to have you working with us."

And so it went, lots of sweet syrup poured down my throat to disguise the bitter taste of the medicine I was being made to swallow.

In actuality, in spite of all of the effort being made to coerce me into the move, it actually was a real promotion and an opportunity to work in a new and very interesting environment. In fact, it would eventually lead me to foreign travel and some real-life "spy" adventures. If all this had just been explained to me beforehand I would have almost surely enthusiastically agreed to the transfer. Alas, that's just not how those two agencies worked in getting what they wanted.

So, more paperwork to sign, and I was becoming an employee of the Central Intelligence Agency. I turned in my NSA badge and would receive a CIA badge shortly after my arrival at the Langley, Virginia headquarters of The Company.

CIA Headquarters was something of a disappointment after working in the NSA monolith. It was less than half the size of the NSA building. The atmosphere there was certainly easier going than at the NSA, though. It was almost collegial in comparison to the much more militaristic style of the NSA. I was always expecting the staff of the NSA to start marching off in close-order drill when it was time to leave work.

When I arrived at the CIA headquarters there were interactions with the

CIA's Housing Assistance Department in order to find me an apartment in Northern Virginia and arrange my move. I had actually acquired a lot more stuff that needed moving during my years in the Laurel, Maryland apartment. Within a few weeks I was living in Reston, Virginia, a very nice planned community about a half hour drive from CIA Headquarters. My new apartment came complete with a swimming pool and lots of young female government employees. The Defense Communications Agency already had a large facility in Reston, and the town was soon to explode with lots more government facilities. Reston was really the place to be for a young ambitious government employee on the make.

I was next enrolled into the comprehensive training program offered by the CIA. I was to go through the same training that was given to all of the intelligence analysts. This would enable me to get a better understanding of their work and help me to design workstation software that would best meet their needs. That actually sounded like lots of fun to me!

It turns out that the job of an intelligence analyst at the CIA differed dramatically from one working for the NSA. The inputs the NSA analyst dealt with were actually pretty straightforward – primarily patterns of communications and other electronic emissions. They didn't break codes, that was done by cryptanalysts with the assistance of specialized computers and software. They simply studied signal patterns. For example, NSA COMINT analysts studied the patterns of communications signals looking for information on why and by whom they were being sent. One of the COMINT intelligence analysts I knew had discovered the existence of an entire North Korean army corps that had previously been unknown just by studying the timing, patterns, and frequency of their radio messages – all without having to actually have any of their messages actually decoded. ELINT and TELINT analysts studied radar and telemetry data to determine how effectively their associated systems worked and probed them for weaknesses that could be exploited. All of these NSA analysts dealt with very specific and relatively limited amounts of data in performing their jobs.

The inputs that a CIA intelligence analyst dealt with were far more varied and far more voluminous. In fact, their main problem at the time was sifting through tons of extraneous information in order to find a few nuggets of valuable information. The problem centered on an inability to always get the right information to the right analyst. Analysts were often buried in information that they had absolutely no interest in seeing, but which might be of incredible interest to another analyst sitting just down the hall from them. Yet, rarely was there any way for them to know this. Thus, the CIA analyst workstation would have to deal with solving very different problems than the NSA workstation.

So, I went through CIA intelligence analyst training classes that started off with simple topics such as basic analytical thinking skills, report writing, and briefing skills. More advanced topics soon followed that covered techniques for analyzing raw intelligence data and trying to make sense of it. How to review a huge amount of seemly innocuous information, discover patterns and relationships buried in it, and derive valuable conclusions from it all. In many ways I imagined it to be similar to detective work.

Then came the really fun part of the training: a trip to The Farm. This was the nickname of a CIA training facility used by the Directorate of Operations - the clandestine part of the CIA that ran real spies in the field. This part of the CIA was quite separate and distinct from the Directorate of Intelligence, where the intelligence analysts worked. At this point in time it had been decided that in order for the intelligence analysts to get some idea of the problems in procuring information from the field, trainees were sent through a mini-course at The Farm. This was to enable them to better understand the difficulties their fellow employees went through to provide them with the information they needed to do their jobs. Alas, to my knowledge, the CIA no longer does this, but I was one of the lucky participants in this program.

The official name of The Farm was Camp Peary and it was located near Williamsburg, Virginia. We trainees were to spend a week there in order to experience just a taste of what the clandestine employees actually did. We would be shown some of the basics of interrogation, surveillance and counter-surveillance, illegal border crossings, dead letter drops, lock picking, bugging a room, document photography, clandestine radio operation, and even get a chance to shoot a few guns. There was even a class called "Flaps and Seals" that dealt with how to surreptitiously open letters and sealed document. This all sounded like a veritable trip to Disneyland for me, but most of the other students seemed to think it all a big waste of time. They were a pretty snobby group and didn't seem to know what to think of me at all. Of course, we weren't allowed to speak to each other regarding any details about our actual jobs at the CIA, but somehow the other intelligence analyst trainees spotted me as something of an odd-duck. I eventually heard that they thought that I was a plant from the Directorate of Security and was actually there to spy on them. It was all such fun and games!

You can't really learn all that much about clandestine operations in just a week, but I really got the bug from the little training I did receive there to actually want get into the field one day and do some real spying. One extremely fortuitous thing that did happen during my week there was my first experience in firing a handgun.

One day a firearms instructor gave us a lecture on shooting a handgun with lots of emphasis on safety, and then took us out to a pistol range and let us shoot a variety of revolvers and pistols. I absolutely loved it and amazingly enough I could actually shoot a handgun with pretty good accuracy. None of the other students could hit the broad side of a barn, but I did remarkably well at it, and it was my very first time even holding a handgun. The firearms instructor told me that I was a natural shooter with a handgun and that I should pursue shooting further. He even suggested I consider taking up shooting as a hobby. He told me about all of the amateur handgun competition matches that were going on in Northern Virginia.

Alas, after the initial excitement of that day's shooting passed, I just let this opportunity pass. I certainly would have been a whole lot better prepared for the day when I would actually have to use a handgun to save my own life if I had taken his suggestions to heart, but more on that later.

Intelligence analyst training completed, it was time to get to work on designing and developing the software for their workstation. I was to be the lead software designer on the project and there were ten other developers assigned to work with me. All of the hardware was to be put together from off-the-shelf components, so the hardware team was only five engineers. We also were getting support from the Directorate of Science and Technology,

It really took me awhile to get my head around the key problem that the workstation had to solve to make it the most useful tool in the analysts' arsenal for making sense of all of the information flowing into the CIA. The analysts themselves were organized into a series of "desks" around specific areas of interest to the CIA. In 1974, the key desks were Soviet Bloc, European, Middle East, South Asia, Asian Pacific, Latin America, and Africa. The Soviet Bloc desk was the largest and most important, since the Cold War was still raging. The workstation was to be prototyped using a select group of their analysts first.

I spent quite a bit of time speaking with analysts before I got my first hint of what the key problem was that they dealt with. It was simply making sure that the right analyst got the right information. They were spending an extraordinary amount of time discarding information that wasn't of any interest to them. If somehow the workstation could automatically sift through the chaff and only show them what was really of interest to them it would save them huge amounts of time and make them hugely more productive. It was this information sifting that the workstation really needed to perform.

Then it came to me, it wasn't discarding unneeded information that was the key function that the workstation should perform, but rather making sure that only appropriate information was shown to an analyst in the first place. It wasn't the workstation that was going to be the key, is was a backend information routing system that would only send information to an analyst that he was actually interested in seeing. After this breakthrough in my thinking the problem actually became simple to solve.

The solution was based on a really simple concept centered around assigning Topics to all bits of raw intelligence data that was going to be made available to the intelligence analysts, and identifying which analysts were interested in each Topic. For example, let's say that that it was reported that the Soviet submarine K-228 had just left Murmansk to start a patrol. George, the analyst specializing in Soviet naval affairs would definitely be interested in knowing this. Harry, who specializes in Soviet economic affairs, could care less about this. So, George would subscribe to the Topics of "Soviet" and "Submarine", and would then get all such messages routed to his workstation. In addition, Mary, who specializes in Soviet nuclear weapons, would also want to know about this, because K-228 was a Yankee class ballistic missile submarine. So, she would subscribe to the Topics of "Soviet" and "Ballistic Missile", and would receive a copy of the same information on her workstation.

But what if Mary was on vacation, or had transferred off the Soviet desk? If all of this logic were coded directly into the software, a programmer would have to update the software, test it to make sure that they hadn't made a mistake in changing the code, and then make sure that the new software was reinstalled on the backend information routing server. Since intelligence analysts were constantly moving around, and even changing their specialties, the need to continuously change the software would soon become a nightmare.

That's where the idea of a rules-based system came in. What if all of the rules for routing intelligence information were stored in a database and not in the program code? The software could read the database to find the most up-to-date rules to use for routing messages. The database containing the rules, now known as the rule base, could easily be updated by anyone, without having to change the software in any way.

That's what we actually implemented. The rule base had a very simple to use maintenance program associated with it that allowed non-technical people, like the intelligence analysts and their bosses, to change it at any time. In addition to information routing rules, it also contained rules for analyzing raw intelligence information entering the system and assigning the proper topics to them. So, for example, any reference to submarine K-228 would result in such topics as "Soviet", "Submarine", "Navy", "Ballistic Missile", etc., being assigned to it and the message then being routed to analysts interested in those Topics based upon routing rules also encoded in the rules base.

It took quite a while to come up with all of the initial Topic rules, but the rest of the system came together pretty easily. We had rough versions of the workstation and backend message routing server up and running in six months. That was in January 1975. We had prototypes being tested by a few of the Soviet Desk analysts by June. By the end of 1975, we had the whole Soviet Desk using the new workstation, and the rest of the desks clamoring for their own. They were a huge hit. A simple rules-based system wasn't exactly artificial intelligence, but it was the closest the Directorate of Intelligence was going to get for quite a few years.

So, in the early part of 1976 I was sitting pretty and being treated like a whiz kid again. I got a promotion, a special award, and got to talk with more big bosses, this time CIA big bosses. I was in such a comfortable position that I actually decided to use this to my advantage. I still remembered what a great time I had at The Farm and working in the field was still a dream of mine. So, I started a lobbying campaign. Every time I got the ear of a higher-up at The Company, I told them how much I wanted to get out of Langley and do something in the field. I had no illusions about joining the real spies of the Directorate of Operations, but still pleaded that there must be something useful that I could do in some foreign country. I was relentless on this topic and brought it up to anyone who I thought could conceivably help to make it happen.

Lo and behold, in early June 1976 I was called into my boss' office. His name was William. He was something of an exception to the preference for employees with Ivy League backgrounds at the CIA. He was an ex-Air Force officer and always sat stiffly upright in his office chair. He was wound pretty tightly, but was actually a pretty decent guy. He said: "Stephen, you're really becoming a royal pain in my ass with all your requests for getting an overseas assignment. What's it going to take to get you to shut up?"

"Just send me on one and I'll be completely out of your hair," I quickly replied, with a slight chuckle.

"OK, you win. The new workstations are working just fine and the existing crew should be able to take care of any maintenance issues that pop up." He then gave me an evil grin and said: "How would you like to go to Iran?".

I knew absolutely nothing about Iran other than that is was in the Middle East, that the Shah was both a key ally and a thorn in our side because of his part in instigating the OPEC oil crisis of 1973 and the subsequent huge price raises for oil. Iran also had the most powerful military in the region and the US was pouring tons of modern weaponry into this country. That was about it.

"Yes, I would love to go to Iran."

"Alright, our friends in the SAVAK, Iran's intelligence service, are clamoring for a computer guru to help them design a system for tracking foreigners in their country. Because of all of your lobbying you're being considered as that guru. You would be working at the Ministry of War Building in Tehran, where the SAVAK is headquartered. You will not be working out of the embassy and will not have diplomatic cover. You won't need it since you'll just be acting as if you were a private US contractor working directly for the Iranian government. Still interested?"

"Absolutely!"

"OK, I'll pass the word upstairs that you actually want this job. I would advise you, though, that I think this a lousy move for your career. Right now you're one of the top dogs in software development for the Directorate of Intelligence. You go off into the hinterlands on some completely unrelated task and the management will soon forget you. Are you really sure you want to do this?"

"Completely sure!"

William shook his head sadly and said: "OK, I've always thought you were a little crazy and I guess this just confirms it. You should hear something in the next few weeks if you're selected for the Iran assignment, and I think you'll actually get it. Sorry to see you go, and good luck with your career."

"Thanks, right now I'm not worried about that. I'm just excited that I'm actually going to get out in the field and see another part of the world."

"Yeah, 'Join the CIA and See The World'. Wait...that's actually a slogan for the Navy, isn't it? Well, anyway, good luck Stephen".

"Thanks, William!"

Just three days later I got the word that I would be going off to Iran. With that I was about to start off on the first real adventure in an otherwise very sheltered life. One that would even briefly take me away from computers and out into the field tracking Soviet activities in Iran. I had absolutely no idea what I was getting myself into!

Of course, I had to be briefed first by the Middle Eastern desk and given a little background information on the environment in Iran. Mainly I was warned not to screw up and not to piss-off anyone at the embassy, the local CIA station, or at the SAVAK. I did find out some interesting information about the SAVAK, though.

SAVAK is an acronym for the Farsi words meaning Organization of Intelligence and National Security. It had been established in 1956 with the help of the CIA and the Israeli Mossad. It had virtually unlimited powers and it mercilessly tracked down, tortured, and executed any opponents of the Shah. It also closely collaborated with the CIA in monitoring Soviet activities within Iran and the surrounding countries. These were the jolly folk I would be soon be working with.

7

OFF TO TEHRAN

Iran itself was the modern nation that had evolved from ancient Persia. The language spoken there was Farsi and in written form it closely resembled Arabic. In fact, Arabic script was used to represent numerals in the written Farsi language. This meant that when I first arrived there I wouldn't even be able to read house numbers until I picked up some basic understanding of Arabic numbers.

Tehran was an extremely modern and cosmopolitan city, yet still had a very ancient bazaar district: the Grand Bazaar. This was an amazing place, and was split into miles of corridors. Each corridor specialized in different types of goods: copper items, gold, carpets, spices, and innumerable other things. Modern goods and appliances were even available there. It was located in the southern part of Tehran and its corridors actually totaled over 6 miles in length.

Tehran had a population of almost 5 million then and was located at about the same altitude as Denver. It sat right at the foot of the snow-capped Alborz mountain range. The climate was semi-arid, with the large central desert located immediately to the south of the city and a mountain range to the north. It was really a gigantic desert oasis. In the summer it was hot and dry, in the winter it was cold but usually stayed above freezing. It rarely snowed in the city in the winter. There were also occasional sandstorms that hit the city and which could be quite dangerous, but no really serious sandstorms hit while I lived there.

Iran at that time was definitely not a conservative Islamic state. There were nightclubs and bars there, and the Iranians made a truly excellent vodka. The city and most of the surrounding country was absolutely exploding with economic activity. The Shah might be a tyrant, but he had done everything he could to catapult Iran into the twentieth century and reestablish it as the dominant economic and military power in the region. The big rise in oil prices that he had helped engineer were providing him with all the capital he needed to do it. The Shah spent money like a drunken sailor on any development project presented to him. He bought nuclear reactors and entire petrochemical plants. He was to even buy over $10 billion dollars of US weapons for his military. Hyperinflation was becoming a problem with so much money being poured into the economy. Women enjoyed equal rights with men, and everyone in the city seemed to have lots of money. Checks and credit cards were almost unheard of but it was not unusual for a businessman to be walking around with $15,000, or even more, in cash, in his pockets.

Alas, the infrastructure of Iran was completely inadequate to support this explosion in economic activity. There weren't enough railroads, highways, airports, or seaports to handle the movement of all the goods now flowing through the economy. Ships waited months to be unloaded in Iran's ports. There were over a million cars on the road in Tehran and traffic had slowed there to a walking pace.

The city itself seemed to almost flow downhill from the north to the south. At the northern part, which was the highest in elevation and where the air was coolest and cleanest, lived the richest and most influential people in the city. Further south were middle-class neighborhoods and Tehran University. Then came an older part of the city where the foreign embassies, the old Parliament, and the Grand Bazaar were located. A little further south took you to a notorious red light district called The Fort. Then came the poorest districts where hoards of new residents flocked into the city and hoped to get a piece of the economic boom for themselves. It featured cramped alleyways and small single-story houses where up to a dozen families might be jammed into a single room. Finally, came the virtual shantytowns. Although nowhere near as impoverished as those in developing nations, these were an ongoing shame to all of those Iranians who were directly benefiting from the country's explosive growth. There seemed to be far too many people being left out of the boom.

I arrived in Tehran in July 1976. By the time I got there the truly insane economic boom that Iran had undergone for the previous few years had finally started to cool down a little, due to a world-wide recession and corresponding drop in demand for oil. Nevertheless, the economy was still growing at a phenomenal rate.

I was put up in a Hilton hotel right in the heart of the downtown and just a short distance from the Ministry of War building. Improbably, right down the street from the hotel was a Kentucky Fried Chicken franchise. It was actually the only US fast food franchise in Iran, but when I first arrived it was a bit of a shock to me to see it there. The rest of the city around the hotel seemed very foreign to me, but very modern with lots of pedestrian traffic and completely insane motor traffic. I couldn't read any of the shop or street signs. However, from my first day there I simply loved this place!

I got directions to the Ministry of War building and walked there my first day at work. I was to ask for a Colonel Namdar when entering the building. He was to be my primary contact while I was working with the SAVAK. He also ended up becoming my landlord and even a good friend. In spite of our friendship, I never called him anything other than "Colonel". Somehow it just seemed right to do so and he appeared to enjoy my addressing him that way.

Colonel Namdar turned out to be a slightly rotund and extremely jolly man wearing an ornate military uniform. He was balding and what was left of his hair was long, stringy, and black. It reminded me of a mop. He spoke impeccable English and was charming, outgoing, and incredibly friendly. He seemed to be continually laughing at what he considered to be the absurdities of life. He immediately brought me to his office and ordered tea for us. He seemed the complete opposite of the kind of man I expected to be working for the notorious SAVAK. I think I expected someone who looked like a Gestapo villain in an old World War II movie. He seemed more like a dark-haired department store Santa Claus. Alas, he would die in the Iranian revolution, doing what he surely felt was his duty to the very last.

I never fully understood all of the Colonel's precise duties. He seemed to have his hand in many of the things that the SAVAK was responsible for doing. The Third Bureau of the SAVAK was responsible for internal security and the Eighth Bureau for counter-intelligence. His responsibilities seemed to span both of these organizations, and some others, too.

"Welcome to Iran, Mr. Connor. Are you alone in our country, or did you bring any family with you?"

"I am alone."

I had many short-term relationships with women during the time leading up to my stay in Iran, but none that had ever developed into anything very serious. My job was really my true love. I loved my work. I loved playing with computers.

My passions outside of work were reading, theater, movies, classical music, and learning of all kinds. I had a voracious appetite for knowledge. I always crushed my opponents in trivia games because my scope of interests was so very broad and I had a terrific memory. I read at least two or three books a month on science, history, or philosophy, with the occasional work of popular fiction thrown into the mix. I felt myself most happy in my own company. I was a true introvert, a nerd, and an intellectual. In other words, virtually impossible for any woman to live with!

"Well then, we must first arrange appropriate housing for you. I have a beautiful house that I would love to offer to you. We must go see it immediately!"

With that he lifted his phone and barked some orders into it in Farsi. He then led me to a side entrance of the building where a Mercedes Benz sedan, complete with uniformed driver, awaited us. Off we went to see the house.

Tehran traffic was simply horrendous, even in the middle of the day. The streets were jammed with Peykans, a locally manufactured compact car. Traffic signals and even lane markings were just considered to be suggestions by drivers. Way too many cars tried to navigate down way too few streets. I regularly saw four lanes of traffic traveling down a three-lane road. A full quarter of all the automobiles in Iran were involved in a traffic accident of some kind every year. Riding here in a car was a thrilling adventure at any time of day.

As we rode in the back of his car Colonel Namdar must have seen the look of shock on my face at the chaos all around us. He laughed and said: "Mr. Connor, I entreat you to never attempt to drive a car yourself while in Iran. You will always have a car and driver at your beck and call while you work for us. All you need do is pick up a phone and call the number I will give you. You will have a car available to you wherever you are within minutes of calling. Is that acceptable to you?" With that he wrote a phone number in English numerals onto a slip of paper in a small notebook, and tore it out and handed it to me.

I took it gratefully and said: "I am certainly happy to promise not to drive here. Thank you so much for your kind offer."

"It is truly my pleasure to offer you this slightest of courtesies. Please feel free to ask anything of me that may be of assistance to you. You are a guest in my country and the Koran says that a guest is a gift from Allah."

At first I thought the Colonel was putting me on, but this was something I was to hear throughout my stay in Iran and see played out in my interactions with virtually all of the Iranians I met. They were deadly serious when it came to their duties as hosts.

Next, the Colonel said: "Oh, but I have been an idiot. I have not inquired as to any preference you may have on where you would like to live. My home is in the Darrous district. Most Americans in Tehran live in another part of the city. Would you prefer to live among your countrymen?"

The Darrous district was one of those in the northern part of the city where the Iranian rich and elite lived. It's still that way, even today.

"No, I would prefer to live in more of an Iranian neighborhood. If I wanted to live with Americans, I would have stayed at home."

The Colonel laughed heartily and said: "Wonderful, I sincerely hope you find my modest house satisfactory."

A short time later we arrived at his "modest house". I can only describe it as something of a small mansion. It had a formal garden with a large pool in the back. It had a beautifully landscaped front yard. It had two bedrooms and a large dining room with marble floors. It had a huge living room that featured a gigantic skylight. It looked like the type of house you might find in Beverly Hills.

"Colonel, this house is amazing, but I think it's going to be too expensive for me."

"Mr. Connor, this house is yours free of charge. You are our guest and we certainly wouldn't charge you money to live here."

Now, my suspicions went on high alert. Why was I, a pretty lowly peon at the CIA being offered a free mini-mansion to live in? What was the motive of the Colonel, or his bosses, in offering it to me? I was becoming very suspicious.

"Perhaps a smaller apartment would be more appropriate for a single man such as myself."

"Nonsense," the Colonel replied. "I could not bear to see you living in such a small home. If this house is not satisfactory to you, we will find you one better." The Colonel was starting to get annoyed. I realized that by refusing what really was an amazing gift I was about to insult him.

"No, no, this house is more than satisfactory. I just don't feel I deserve it. I'm not going to be doing enough for you and your country to earn such a wonderful home."

"Don't be absurd," the Colonel said again. "You are my guest and I insist that this is the humblest abode I would be comfortable in seeing you live. If you are concerned about maintaining the home, be assured that you will have a housekeeper and gardener. You need to do nothing other than enjoy yourself while living here."

And so I ended up living in the nicest, most luxurious home of my entire life - and rent-free to boot!

The Colonel next took me back to the hotel to get my things. He then drove me back to the house, where I finally met my housekeeper, Homa. She helped me unpack. Homa was probably in her early 50's and was built like a shot putter. She amply filled the light blue housekeeper's uniform she always wore.

She claimed to speak no English, but didn't need to. She marvelously anticipated my every need and worked tirelessly to keep everything in the house spic and span. You could eat off of any floor in the house. She magically appeared every morning, except for Friday and Saturday, which was the weekend in Iran.

Pretty much everything was closed on Friday, since it was considered a day devoted to prayer. I worked at SAVAK Headquarters from Sunday through Thursday.

Homa left each day in the early evening, after serving me dinner and cleaning up afterward. She was undoubtedly a SAVAK agent or informer ordered to keep watch over me, but I was more than willing to put up with that since she was such a fantastic housekeeper.

I never even learned the name of my gardener. He was an elderly Iranian who simply appeared a few times every week while I was at work and kept the gardens in immaculate condition. There was never even a blade of grass out of place in my yard.

I also had a car and driver appear at my doorstep every workday at 7:30 AM to take me to SAVAK Headquarters. After work, I simply requested a car and would be driven home. At night or on weekends I could just telephone for a car and one would appear no later than 30 minutes after I called.

If for some reason I chose not to use an official car and driver, I could always take a taxi. Taxis were plentiful. There were two types in Tehran: taxis that could be called for by phone to drive you to a particular location, and taxis that ran fixed routes and were hailed on the street. The fixed route taxis were way cheaper than the on-call taxis and were also far more numerous. If I wanted to catch a taxi from the Ministry of War building, I just stood in front and hailed one. It would slow down and I would shout out the name of the street on which I lived. If the driver was going that way he would nod affirmatively and I would get into the cab. He might also pick up other riders along his route and sometimes the little Peykan cab would be completely full of passengers.

Now it took me a while to make sense of Iranian nodding. Iranians don't shake their heads "no". To indicate a "no", they nod their heads up. To indicate a "yes", they nod their heads down. I was involved in many comical misunderstandings until I finally figured this out.

Now, as for conversing with cab drivers or fellow passengers, this could be a problem for me. Since I was so suddenly sent to Iran I never had any time to attend one of the CIA's excellent language training courses. Everyone I worked with at SAVAK Headquarters spoke impeccable English, so there was little motivation for me to learn much Farsi. During my time in Iran I only picked just up enough "street Farsi" to accomplish the most minimal communication with shopkeepers and cab drivers.

Most Iranians I encountered on the street did not speak English. Strangely enough, a surprising number spoke at least a little French. Since I'm not aware of any particularly strong French presence in Iran during its history I've never figured out why that was so. In fact, the most common way that Iranians said "thank you" to each other was to use the French word "merci". So, many times my French enabled me to make up for my total lack of knowledge of Farsi and still communicate with at least some Iranians who didn't speak English.

My quest to get a phone installed in my new home gave me my first inkling of the power of the SAVAK in Iran. Tehran was growing so fast at the time, and the phone system so overloaded, that it normally took up to a year to get a new phone installed. Since this was 1976, there were no cell phones. If you didn't have a landline phone in your house, you would have to walk down the street to a local shop and use a pay phone. So, I went to my local post office (the post office ran the Iranian phone system) and requested a phone be installed in my house. I was told that it would take a year. I happened to mention this to the Colonel one day at work. He just about popped a blood vessel, picked up his phone, and rattled of a string of loud agitated Farsi to whomever he was speaking with. He then hung up the phone with a satisfied look on his face.

"Your phone will be installed tomorrow. Homa will supervise the installation. Let her know where in the house you would like the phone installed, and please, in future talk to me immediately if you have any problems with being properly served by anyone in my country."

That night, through some inventive pantomime I let Homa know where I wanted the phone to go. Sure enough, when I came home the next day I had a telephone. Obviously the SAVAK had some real pull over just about everyone in Iran. This was actually just the first instance of my realizing what a powerful position I had in this country. If you have to live in a police state, it's very good to work for the police.

My next task was to check in at the embassy, and especially the local CIA Station located there. I dropped by and first went through the formality of registering with the embassy as a US citizen residing in a foreign country. I gave them my address and phone number and place of employment. My place of employment automatically raised some eyebrows and I was soon talking to a member of the ambassador's staff, a Mr. Jones. He was dressed in a very conservative diplomatic outfit – a dark gray suit, pale blue shirt, and black and white striped tie.

"So, you are the Stephen Connor we were warned about."

"Warned about?"

"Sorry, I meant informed about. We were informed that you were coming to Tehran and would be assisting our friends at the Parts Company."

"The Parts Company?"

"Oh, you haven't heard that nickname yet, have you? Yes, the very word 'SAVAK' is quite frightening to most Iranian citizens and so when we discuss the SAVAK, especially when in public, we've taken to referring to them as the Parts Company. I don't know how that term actually originated, but it now has taken on a life on of its own. Anyway, all I want to do now is to emphasize what I'm sure you were already told back home – the Shah is a vital ally of the US and the Parts Company is an important organization for keeping him in power. I know that you are just doing some computer consulting for them, but please don't do anything that could embarrass the US while working there. Just do your job the best you can and otherwise keep a low profile. Understood?"

"Very clearly," I said.

I also briefly visited the CIA Station while at the embassy, but they were too busy to speak with a lowly minion such as myself and just gave me a quick word about not screwing up anything and not bringing any unpleasant attention or embarrassment to the CIA while I was in Iran. With that, they said goodbye and good luck to me and then scurried back to their much more important work.

My job with the SAVAK turned out to be trivially easy. The SAVAK already had all the resources they needed to get the job done on their own. They even owned their own computer company, Isiran, which imported and distributed mainframe computers into the country. Isiran performed translations of all of the mainframe software into Farsi. They even manufactured a Farsi computer terminal.

The software development team the SAVAK had put together was absolutely world-class. Everyone on the team had a master's degree or PhD in computer science or business administration. At least ten members of the team were very experienced, and very highly paid, systems engineering and software consultants from the US or England. They must have had a total of over one hundred people working on this project. I met most of them during my stay in Iran, but not all.

They already had a detailed plan put together for the network architecture they would need to implement this system and had some very high-powered mainframes up and running. All they really wanted was somebody from the CIA who claimed to be an expert to say that everything they were doing was A-OK. That's about all that I did. I attended daily progress meetings and signed-off on all of their plans. Rarely was I able to contribute anything more valuable. It soon actually became pretty boring.

In addition to the overall job being kind of boring, there was a whole cultural issue that I had to deal with there. In Iran, there seemed to be absolutely no sense of urgency in any governmental or business initiative. Every meeting started off with tea and snacks and extended conversations about how everyone's life was going and how their families were doing. At least half or more of the time allocated to any meeting was burned up in socializing. This was a very different world from the high-pressure environments in which I was used to working.

In addition, there was the Iranian concept of "farad". Literally, this Farsi word meant "tomorrow". In actuality what it really meant was some far distant time in the future, one that you really needn't worry about. Whenever I would inquire about the need to accomplish some specific project task expeditiously, I would always hear: "Don't worry about that, we will do that farad".

The project itself was pretty straightforward. Among its many responsibilities, the SAVAK ran the Iranian Border Police under the overall command of the Third Bureau. Their responsibilities were similar to our Customs and Immigration services.

The system they were building would have computer terminals installed in every port of entry into Iran, whether the travelers were arriving by air, train, road, or sea. Foreigners would have their passport and visa information entered into the system and it would be stored in a large database on a mainframe computer. In addition, every time one of the foreigners checked into a hotel, they were required by law to surrender their passport each night at the front desk. In the middle of the night, a Border Police officer would drop by each hotel to inspect and write down the information from each guest's passport. At the end of his shift he would take this information to a Border Police station and then it would be used to update the system as to each foreigner's current location. Foreigners who resided in Iran on a more long-term basis were required to register their addresses with the Border Police. Any other official interactions with a foreigner could also be entered into the system and the database updated. Thus the SAVAK would be able to keep very close track of all foreigners in Iran. The system also was built to allow the storage of additional information on people the SAVAK wanted to keep a particularly close eye on – like Soviet block "tourists" and diplomatic staff, or foreigners suspected of harboring anti-Shah opinions. Terminals for entering this information were located at the SAVAK headquarters.

So, with all this in mind, I went and visited the Colonel one day after I had been working there for about a year. He was always happy to see me and when we finally dispensed with tea, snacks, and a lengthy conversation about family, I was finally able to get to the real point of my meeting with him.

"Colonel, the project is going extremely well, but I don't think I'm working hard enough for you," I said to him.

The Colonel appeared shocked to hear this. "Nonsense, I hear nothing but compliments about your work for us. The team feels that you are simply invaluable. If anything, they are already worrying about the day you will be leaving us."

"Frankly, Colonel, I have quite a bit of time on my hands. I feel like there is much more I could be doing to keep busy."

The Colonel laughed and said, "Ah, you Americans, you always seem to want to work yourselves to death, and do it quickly at that. Relax and enjoy your time with us and live your life as it was meant to be lived."

"Well, Colonel, isn't there something else I might get involved in while here working for you? I know, for example, that one of your responsibilities is working with the Eighth Bureau to keep close tabs on Soviet-bloc diplomats and personnel. I would love to be able to learn more about the work you are doing here."

The Colonel gave me a very suspicious look at this point. I could almost see the gears turning in his head. Who was I, really? I was supposed to be a computer consultant, but I was after all with the CIA. Did I actually have some hidden agenda? Was I there to spy on the Colonel and the work he was doing? Had he not been viewing me with enough suspicion? What was I really doing in Iran?

This is what it's like when you work for any kind of intelligence organization. It's like being <u>trapped in a hall of mirrors</u>. Your vision of reality is severely distorted. Many of the images you see aren't real, and there may very well be sinister things lurking behind them. You can't take anything at face value, you have to constantly be on your guard and deal with everyone as a possible threat. Trust no one!

So, after some thought the Colonel finally said, "Well, I had no idea that you might be interested in our humble work in this area. Of course, I would be happy to brief you about it."

Now I really bore down on the Colonel, "More than being briefed, I would love to actually see what you are doing in the field. Would it be possible to tag along with some of your men as they do their work? In the United States we have the concept of a 'ride-along'. This is an opportunity for civilians to ride along in a police car and observe the actual work a police officer does during his shift. Would something along those lines be possible for me, but with your people?"

Well, I'd really gone and done it! I was way out of bounds in making this request and it would likely to get me into huge trouble with the local CIA station if they found out about it. I was doing exactly the opposite of what I had been told to do, but damn it, here was a chance to see some actual intelligence work as it was happening. I was sticking my neck way out, but I felt it was worth the risk. After all, what was the worst thing that could happen to me? I could be sent home in disgrace and put back to work on some other computer system - just how bad could that be? What the heck, nothing ventured, nothing gained!

I thought it would be "farad" until I got an answer to my request, but the Colonel surprised me. "Certainly, if you are interested in seeing what we are doing in this area, then I would be most honored to accommodate your wishes. I will have my Captain Rahbar contact you and make all the necessary arrangements. Will that be satisfactory?"

"Very satisfactory," I said. "Oh, one additional favor I would ask of you is that you don't bring this up with your CIA contacts, if that wouldn't be a problem for you".

With that the Colonel actually broke out into a huge laugh. "Ah, I see that you may be much more of a rogue than I ever realized. Of course, this will remain our little secret." He brought his finger up to his mouth in a "shhh motion" and then laughed again. We then lapsed back into social conversations about the weather, family, and other trivia. Finally the Colonel excused himself and got up to leave his office. I left with him and returned to my office. I had really done it now! Looking back on what I had done, I can't believe I acted so rashly. Well, I was still only 29 years old and had lots more to learn about the harsh realities of life.

That evening at home, my phone rang. I answered it and heard a clear, strong voice with a slight British accent say: "Good evening, Mr. Connor. This is Captain Rahbar calling. Is this a convenient time for us to speak?"

With real excitement I replied: "Why, yes Captain, of course. It's a pleasure to hear from you so soon."

"Would it be convenient for me to drop by your home this evening to discuss the request you made to Colonel Namdar?"

Uh oh, was I in trouble or was this going to be a friendly conversation? Well, there was only one way to find out.

"It would be great if you could drop by tonight. When would you like to come over?"

The Captain replied: "I can be there in a half hour, if that will be acceptable to you?"

"That would be great. I look forward to meeting you."

"Very good, I will see you shortly, then."

With that he hung up. Well, what ever happened, it promised to be interesting. Homa had just left, but the house was immaculate, as usual. I quickly checked out the pantry and set out some of the sweet pastries that were so popular in Iran. I also made a pot of coffee and got water into my teakettle. Whether Captain Rahbar preferred coffee or tea I wanted to be prepared. Was I nervous? Nah – I was terrified! I had visions of the Captain arriving with a squad of armed men and dragging me off to the dreaded SAVAK Evin prison. Conditions were supposed to have somewhat improved there in recent years, but it still reputed to be a real hellhole.

Exactly 30 minutes after he called, there was a knock at my door. I opened it to find an Iranian man in his early 30s standing there, wearing an expensive looking brown leather bomber jacket and Levi jeans. He had jet-black hair and a thin black mustache. He looked like nothing like a Captain in the SAVAK. From his appearance I would have guessed that he was a young nightclub owner. I wondered if he had bell-bottoms at home and listened to psychedelic rock every night. He looked very stylish, indeed, and wore a large gold ring on his right hand.

He queried: "Mr. Connor?"

"Yes," I said while furtively looking around him for any sign of the dreaded squad of armed men. None were visible. "Please come in." I held out my hand and he shook it firmly.

He stepped inside and scanned the interior of my home with very attentive dark eyes. I invited him into the living room and offered to hang up his jacket.

"No thank you, I prefer to leave it on."

Was he armed under that jacket? I'd bet he was. I offered him coffee or tea and cookies. He accepted coffee, asking for it black, and declined the other two. He continued to scan my house with very alert eyes. I went into the kitchen, poured two cups of coffee, and put them down on the low coffee table in my living room.

Captain Rahbar then said: "Well Mr. Connor, exactly what can I do for you?"

"I would like to have a chance to see firsthand something of your surveillance operations against Soviet-bloc personnel. I don't want to get in your way, but I would love to see your teams in action. Would that be possible, Captain?"

He stared rather intently at me at first, and then seemed to relax just a little. He said: "Please call me Jake. It's a nickname I picked up while studying in England. Yes, I think we can arrange something that won't disrupt our operations. The Soviets know they are being watched. I see very little harm coming from your observing our operations. When would you like to do it?"

"I have meetings to attend every afternoon, so it would need to be in the morning or in the evening after work."

Jake said: "Well today is Tuesday, how about I pick you up from your office at 8:30 AM this Thursday and give you a tour then?"

"That would be perfect," I replied.

And so the game was afoot!

8

I REALLY PUT MY FOOT IN IT

I could hardly wait for Thursday to arrive. The next day I made sure that my calendar was completely clear for Thursday morning. Nothing was going to stand in the way of my big chance to see SAVAK field agents in operation. I still harbored some doubts on whether it would really happen, but I did everything I could to make it possible.

Sure enough, at exactly 8:30 AM on Thursday morning, I looked up from the desk to see Jake standing in my office doorway. He was dressed similarly to the night I saw him at my home, but with the addition of a very dark pair of aviator sunglasses.

He smiled and said: "Well, Mr. Connor, are you ready for your ride-along?" He laughed when I blushed at being reminded of how I had phrased my original request to the Colonel.

Hoping to cover my embarrassment, I quickly replied: "If I'm to call you Jake, then you must call me Stephen. Please, no more Mr. Connor."

"Certainly, Stephen," Jake said, still grinning.

Then off we went. We left from a back entrance of the Ministry building and got into an awaiting Peykan. It was gray in color and looked pretty beat up. A driver sat in it, wearing the very same aviator sunglasses as Jake's, but was just wearing a white t-shirt and jeans. Jake and I slipped into the back seat. The battered Peykan quickly pulled out into the crazy Tehran traffic. The throbbing sound of the motor and the car's amazingly quick acceleration immediately clued me into the fact that this car was a lot more than some old jalopy. It was certainly meant to look like a heap, but there was some serious horsepower under its hood.

We careened along through the Tehran traffic and in about a half hour stopped at a large metal garage door in the middle of a block. Magically the door opened as we rolled up to it and we pulled into a very large garage filled with all kinds of vehicles – cars, large trucks, vans, even a Mercedes stretch limousine. Jake got out and said: "Please follow me, Stephen."

I did as instructed and we stepped out onto the sidewalk and headed up the street. Upon reaching an apartment building at the end of the block, we entered through its lobby. The building itself was four stories tall and had a doctor's office on the first floor. We rode the elevator up to the fourth floor.

The entire top three floors of the building were being used by the SAVAK for monitoring the Soviet embassy complex. The doctor's office on the first floor was strictly a cover to help mask the flow of people into and out of the building. There really were no patients. I don't even think there was a doctor there, either.

Exiting the elevator, we turned right and walked down the hall to a doorway. Jack knocked four times and the door opened. I walked into an apartment that had been turned into an observation post. The windows faced a cross street to the one we had walked up. Near the front windows stood two tripods. They were far enough inside the apartment to not be visible to anyone looking in from outside. One had a telescope similar to a spotting scope you might see at a rifle range. Next to it a 35mm camera with a long lens sat on top of the other tripod. Glancing around I saw three men, all in their 20s and dressed causally like blue-collar workers. There was a radio set against the left wall of the room. I also saw a large table on which walkie-talkies, binoculars, and a movie camera with a large lens all sat.

Jake introduced me to the men. As usual, I immediately forgot their names, as I do whenever I'm introduced to more than one person at a time. He then said: "Take a look at our view".

I looked down Churchill Street (renamed after the Revolution) and from the angle we had I saw the end of a very impressive large building to the right with a hammer and sickle on its end wall. Across the street from it were a couple of two-story buildings that also had emblems and flags of the Soviet Union on their facades. Right in front of them was one of the little kiosks that you see all over Tehran that sell tea, snacks, and soft drinks. You couldn't quite see the front of the large building on our right from our angle, but you certainly could clearly see everyone who entered or left it.

Jake then said: "The big building on the right is the Soviet embassy. The two buildings on the left are the consulate and the Soviet Club. Only Russians are allowed in the Soviet Club - no Iranians. In spite of that bit of mystery surrounding it we think it's actually pretty harmless. It contains a movie theater and music rooms. They show Soviet films four times a week to the embassy staff and other Russian personnel here in Tehran to keep them from being corrupted by having to watch capitalist films. They hold regular concerts in the music rooms and it also has a large bookstore. Apparently the Russians are starved of books in the Soviet Union itself, so the bookstore seems to be the most popular part of the club."

"The consulate next to it primarily issues visas for travel to the Soviet Union. It has a staff of five, four of whom are members of the KGB's First Chief Directorate, 8th Department - that is Foreign Intelligence, and the department within it that is responsible for Iran, Afghanistan, and Turkey. General Kryuchkov is head of the First Chief Directorate, General Polonik head of the 8th Department, and Colonel Lezhnin head of the Iranian desk, or am I boring you with information you already know?"

I smiled at this obvious attempt to somewhat surreptitiously find out if I really knew more than I had been letting on, and replied noncommittally: "No, please continue."

"The consulate is open from 8:00 AM until 2:30 PM and the poor KGB agents actually have to work during that time issuing visas. The fifth non-KGB staff member does all of the paperwork for them, though. The rest of the time they are free to float about the city, causing whatever mischief they may be able to accomplish. Of course, we follow them everywhere, and of course, they know it. They are actually quite courteous to my men. They must realize that if they try anything truly annoying they will likely find themselves in a serious traffic accident, or maybe even being mugged by hooligans." With that, Jake gave me a huge grin.

"So, this is the great game we play here. Oh, you see that kiosk selling soft drinks? Right in front of the consulate and directly across the street from the main embassy entrance? That's ours also. My staff, some of who have been serving there for many years, man it. It's equipped with cameras and radios and is the only business open around here on weekends and holidays. It's hugely popular with the Russians and their purchases actually help defray my budget. Some of the Russians have even become quite friendly with the staff there."

"We also have a fleet of vehicles available to us. You saw some of them in the garage where we parked. There are others parked in all of the streets surrounding the embassy and in radio contact with our watchers. If anyone of interest to us leaves the embassy or consulate, the appropriate cars are contacted and they pick up the subjects for surveillance."

Jake then grinned again, and said: "So, Stephen what do you think of our little setup here?"

I was frankly amazed by the huge amount of the resources the SAVAK had devoted to watching the Russians. This was an immense operation. I asked Jake: "Aren't you duplicating work that's also being done here by the CIA?"

He laughed out loud. "No, your compatriots are too busy with other things to waste time watching the Russians moving about the city. You leave that simple chore to us. We just keep you updated on anything interesting we discover. Other than that you seem remarkably unconcerned about our Russian friends here. I think you mainly like to spy on us."

He gave me another giant grin, and so I wasn't sure if he was being serious or just joking. Just then, one of his men, who was looking through the telescope, said something to Jake and pointed at the consulate building. Jake hastily picked up two sets of binoculars and handed me one pair. He then said: "Well, look what we have here. Viktor should be busy issuing visas, and yet there he is leaving the consulate. I wonder what he's up to today?"

I put the binoculars to my eyes and soon found the man to whom Jake was pointing. Right now he was blinking because the sun was in his eyes and he was fishing inside his jacket for a set of sunglasses. He had a definite Slavic appearance and wore a dark gray double-breasted suit, tan shirt, and a brown tie. After finding his sunglasses and putting them on, he started striding towards us. Upon reaching the corner he hailed a cab and got into it.

Jake motioned to the radio operator who spoke into the microphone. A rapid reply in Farsi soon boomed out of the radio's speakers. Jake then turned to me and said: "Two of our cars have picked up the cab, and a third car will soon be traveling down a street parallel to their path. We won't lose him."

He then continued thoughtfully: "That man is Viktor Avilov. He's definitely KGB. It's extremely unusual for him to be leaving the consulate during normal working hours. I wonder what he's up to?"

We waited in the apartment for almost an hour before we finally heard back from the surveillance team that was following Viktor. It turned out that he had gone to see a dentist! So much for arch KGB conspiracies!

That was how I first met Viktor, and how I set in motion a fantastic chain of events that was to shake the local KGB Residence to its very foundations. You see, in my naiveté I had kicked over a wasp's nest that would cause many people to be stung – even me, eventually – and had absolutely no idea of what I had just done.

The problem was that my friend Jake was actually a paid KGB agent. He had been recruited many years ago while a student in England and his career in the SAVAK had been carefully guided by the KGB.

Jake was feeling very uncomfortable about what was now going on. This strange CIA employee who had no business in doing so was poking around in his domain. The more and more he thought about it, the more nervous he became.

So, shortly after our brief time together, he sent out an emergency request for a meeting with his KGB handler - something he had never had to do before. He made sure that his worst surveillance team was assigned to watch his handler so that this KGB officer could slip away from the watchers and meet Jake secretly. After they spoke, the KGB man was even more concerned than Jake was. He put on a brave face for Jake and tried to calm him down, but inside he was even more upset than Jake. He did, however, tell Jake that he was to temporarily cease all contact with the KGB until the matter could be resolved. This would be a major loss of important intelligence for the KGB, but Jake's connection to them had to be immediately cut before it might lead to his arrest and interrogation by the SAVAK's Third Bureau.

You have to look at the situation from their side: here was this technician from the CIA who was just supposed to be helping build a pretty straightforward computer system for the SAVAK. After sitting on his rear end for an entire year, all of a sudden, completely out of the blue, he asks to check out SAVAK surveillance of the KGB. There was no way that this could be an innocent request. There was absolutely no reason for me to make such a request if I was who I said I was - a simple computer technician. Therefore, I must be something much more dangerous to the KGB. The fact that I arranged to observe the work of one of their most important and trusted agents immediately made me an extremely dangerous threat to the KGB.

Keeping up to date on exactly how they were being watched by the SAVAK was vital to the KGB if they were to accomplish any clandestine work whatsoever in Iran. I obviously must know something was rotten with Jake, but what else did I know? I must be a CIA counter-intelligence agent and I could be getting dangerously close to blowing up their whole operation in Iran. They had to move fast to find out what I knew and to contain any damage I had already done. Who else of their agents in Iran might have been compromised? That's what it all looked like to them from their side of the hall of mirrors.

Information on me was sent on to Moscow for further analysis by the KGB's Second Chief Directorate staff, who were responsible for counter-intelligence. I'm sure they found nothing useful, because there was nothing sinister for them to find. This undoubtedly make me appear even more dangerous – the fact that I appeared so innocent. The CIA must have gone to extraordinary lengths to create such an effective cover me for me. So, I must be extremely important to the CIA.

This is how intelligence organizations around the world, including ours, work. They sometimes build suspicion upon supposition until they have a tower of complete nonsense that they have so artfully and logically created. That's the story of how all of Saddam Hussein's nonexistent weapons of mass destruction came to be created by US intelligence. As for me, I was fast turning into a real nemesis of the KGB.

Then just two months later, an even more disastrous thing happened to the KGB in Iran. One of the top Generals in Iran was a man named Admed Mogharebi. He was very close to the Shah and was extremely influential within the Iranian military. He also had close ties with the CIA and even owned a home in the US. His children went to school in the US. He had also been an active KGB agent since the 1950s.

Jake worked for the Eighth Bureau of the SAVAK – the counter-espionage arm of the agency responsible for watching over the Soviets. The Third Bureau was responsible for internal security. Although he did not have any first-hand knowledge of the activities of the Third Bureau, Jake had given the KGB information on all of the radio frequencies that the SAVAK used for mobile communications between their cars and their bases. Thus the KGB had been listening in on all of the Third Bureau's mobile communications for years from a communications center located on the sixth floor of their embassy. Somehow the Third Bureau figured this out and started practicing strict radio silence within their most important surveillance activities. They continued just enough other radio traffic to keep the KGB from becoming suspicious. Suddenly the Soviets were no longer being regularly informed about the most important targets of surveillance by the Third Bureau.

The Third Bureau had been keeping General Mogharebi under observation for years. Because of his powerful position in the military and close friendship with the Shah they had to treat him with kid gloves. Nevertheless they had strong suspicions that he was working with the Soviets. In May 1977 the General went for a visit to his home in the US. While out of the county, SAVAK Third Bureau teams searched his house and found some pretty suspicions items there. After he returned to Iran the Third Bureau kept his home under extremely close observation by a large team that practiced complete radio silence.

In September 1977, the KGB made a huge mistake. Unaware of the SAVAK's very close surveillance of the General, Boris Kabanov, one of the KGB First Chief Directorate agents working out of the Soviet Embassy, had his driver take him to the General's house in an automobile known to be owned by the Soviets. Upon their arrival, General Mogharebi left his house, supposedly to walk his dog. Kabanov then got out of his car, walked by him, and used a "brush pass" technique to quickly pass him an envelope.

This was all the SAVAK needed. They quickly swarmed onto the scene in great numbers. The General was immediately arrested and taken away to Evin Prison for interrogation. He would soon confess everything.

Kabanov had barely made it back to his car before SAVAK cars surrounded it. Although he brandished his diplomatic passport at the agents and refused to unlock his car's doors, the Third Bureau agents just smashed its windows and dragged Kabanov and his driver out and arrested them both. They would shortly be released, only to be taken directly to the airport and expelled from Iran. That was to be the end of Boris Kabanov's career with the First Chief Directorate. He had been burned and was now useless for continuing in that role.

This was a complete catastrophe for the KGB. Within the last two months their successful penetration of the SAVAK's Eighth Bureau seemed to have been compromised and now they had just lost their most important agent in Iran, and had one of their key officers expelled. The KGB's Lubyanka headquarters staff in Moscow was furious and demanding answers. General Mogharebi had been a vital asset for over 20 years and suddenly he had been arrested. What was going on in Iran?

Of course, in their minds it all pointed back to me. I was the most obvious anomaly visible in the Iranian intelligence scene. All of this had happened right after I suddenly expressed an interest in surveillance of the Soviet embassy. Obviously I must have something to do with initiating both of these calamities. The file the KGB file kept on me was now growing at a prodigious rate. My photo was being handed around all the KGB outposts in Iran and filed away in Moscow. I was clearly a menace to their clandestine operations in Iran. I had to be stopped!

Of course, I was completely oblivious to all of this. I read about General Mogharebi's arrest in the newspaper with some interest, but that was about the extent of my involvement. I had my brief adventure into the operational world of spies with my ride-along with Jake but had now gone back to my regular daily job of project status meetings. I had no idea that I had done anything to raise the ire of the KGB. I was just happy that I hadn't gotten into any trouble with the CIA for "leaving the reservation" and poking my nose into affairs I had no business in doing. I was carefree and content and innocent as a newborn babe.

Shortly after the General's arrest, Jake disappeared. The SAVAK was greatly concerned for a while and mounted a major effort to find out what happened to him. To this day, no one has been able to figure out whether he had been given asylum in the Soviet Union, fled Iran on his own, or just disappeared for some other unrelated reason. The Colonel mildly mentioned it to me one day during one of our normal meetings.

The Colonel said: "Were you aware that our friend Captain Rahbar seems to have disappeared?"

I was startled to hear this and honestly answered: "No, I didn't. What happened?"

"No one seems to know. He simply stopped coming to work one day without warning. One of his men went to his house, entered it, and found it to be empty. All seemed normal in the house, nothing appeared to be disturbed or missing. His car was in the garage. It's a real mystery."

"Wow," was all I could say.

The Colonel looked me in the eye intently and said: "Did you notice anything out of place in his demeanor during your visits with him?"

"I hardly knew him, and so am not sure what would be out of place – but no, I don't think so. He seemed to be a very friendly man, very competent in the work I saw him doing. No, I didn't notice anything odd about him."

"Very well," replied the Colonel, with a somewhat perturbed look on his face. "I'm sure this matter will soon be resolved and some reasonable explanation discovered." Alas, it was not to be. Jake – what ever became of you?

9

THE PEOPLE BECOME UNSETTLED

Of course, all during this time the overall political situation in Iran was rapidly deteriorating, but no one seemed to notice. Everyone was convinced that the Shah was in a rock-solid position as undisputed leader of Iran. By everyone, I mean everyone. Even the KGB had concluded that the Shah was completely secure in his position and had recommended that the Soviet government try to improve relations with him. After all, he had the complete backing of the US, he had tons of money, he had the largest military force in the region, he had the SAVAK actively seeking out and crushing all possible opposition – what could possibly go wrong?

The first problem was that, unknown to anyone but a very few in the royal court, the Shah had been diagnosed with cancer. His days were certainly numbered and there was really no clear path for his succession. Even the Shah felt that his son was too young and inexperienced to take over the throne from him. So, the Shah was just getting sicker and weaker each month.

Next, the benefits of the economic explosion that had occurred had been distributed very unevenly through Iranian society. A full half of Iranians were still illiterate, in spite of vast sums being spent on education. Schools couldn't be built fast enough, teachers trained fast enough. In fact, there was a desperate shortage of skilled workers throughout the economy. The Shah was attempting to move what had been a fundamentally medieval society into the 20th century at an impossibly fast pace.

The Shah himself was completely baffled by what he saw as a complete indifference by the public towards all of the material progress and the new worldwide prestige he had brought to his nation. His people seemed more frustrated by all of the problems brought on by the country's boom than pleased by any of the economic gains he had brought them. They seemed to be suffering from extreme "future shock". Even the upper classes were unsure of Iran's future. Up to $100 million of capital was flowing out of the country each month into overseas banks.

Of course, I lived in a bubble that effectively shielded me from all this social turmoil. The Colonel had actually become a real friend. I still wonder why he chose to do so. He simply seemed to genuinely like me for some unknown reason.

I regularly visited his home and attended lavish parties there. All of his guests were fed mountains of wonderful food. There I met senior government officials, wealthy business people, and even entertainers who were famous in Iran. Most of the entertainers would be coaxed into impromptu performances during the parties and I got to see and hear first hand some of Iran's beautiful and unique music and dance culture.

All of the Colonel's guests treated me with incredibly generous hospitality, even though I was effectively a real nobody in their eyes. The Iranian ideal of treating a guest as a gift from Allah was still a vital part of life there. The chief justice in Iran's highest court even invited me to accompany him on his private plane for a visit to Isfahan, his hometown, after I admitted to him that I hadn't been there yet. I also took a couple of vacations and short weekend trips to Egypt and Europe. I was living the high-life and was completely clueless as to what was really going on in Iran and how the people felt about what was happening to their country.

I experienced the same level of hospitality during my interactions with the everyday people I encountered on the streets of Tehran. They were all incredibly friendly and greeted me with a smile and best wishes whenever I passed by them. Cab drivers invariably offered me a cigarette when I rode in the their cabs (I did smoke back then, just about everyone did), and I would return the favor by offering them an American cigarette. We couldn't speak each other's language, but we could enjoy sharing a smoke together and somehow feeling a real sense of temporary comradery. In spite of whatever tensions were going on just under the surface, all of the people I encountered were universally friendly and generous to me.

I loved the excitement and vibrancy of the streets of Tehran. I loved the smell and taste of the street food and the food served in the hundreds of little local restaurants. Chelo Kabob was pretty much the national dish when I lived there and it tasted simply wonderful to me. Unique to Iran, it was made from ground lamb flattened and then grilled on skewers. It was then served on top of buttered saffroned Persian rice, flat bread, and grilled tomatoes. It tasted divine! Caviar was also cheap and plentiful, and probably the highest quality in the world at that time. It was typically served in large bowls over ice. Iran is the only place I have ever been where I could say: "No, please, no more caviar. I can't eat any more."

Nevertheless, by late in 1977 I was actually starting to get an inkling that all was not well in Iran. It had nothing to do with any shrewd analysis on my part of the Iranian political scene. No, it was a lot simpler than that. It was the questions that I was suddenly getting from a growing number of my colleagues at work, many of whom were top officials within the SAVAK. Questions like:

"Where is the best place to live in the US?"
"What is the best bank in the US?"
"How much does a home cost in the US?"
"How much money does it take to live comfortably in the US?"
"What does a nice car cost in the US?"
"Where are the best schools in the US?"
"Where is the best shopping in the US?"
"Where is the crime rate lowest in the US?"

So, there were a whole lot of questions being asked of me about living in the US. Why? If everything was really hunky dory here in Iran, why was I getting besieged with questions about living in the US from the same people who were responsible for seeing that the Shah's reign was secure? What was up with that? It seemed to me that all of my SAVAK colleagues were starting to make serious plans to move to the US, and to do it quite soon.

Like the good loyal CIA employee I was, I went to the embassy and asked to speak with someone at the CIA Station there. I wanted to report my concerns. I was ushered into the Station and presented with the very most junior officer they could find. This unfortunate fellow had been tasked to listen to my ravings. My concerns were duly noted, I was figuratively patted on the head and told not to bother my little brain anymore about these matters, and politely, but firmly, told to get back to work and stop bothering the adults. Luckily, the absurd concerns I expressed were actually written down in a report and duly filled away. That fact would have a huge impact on my career with the CIA and even one day get me into the White House for a brief visit.

In October of 1977 there were violent demonstrations by students in the city of Qom, less then 80 miles from Tehran. Nevertheless, on December 31, the newly elected President of the United States, Jimmy Carter, made a brief visit to Tehran. In front of TV cameras he made the following toast to the Shah: "Iran, because of the great leadership of the Shah, is an island of stability in one of the more troubled areas of the world. This is a great tribute to you, your Majesty, and to your leadership and to the respect and admiration and love which your people give to you."

In January 1978 there were more violent riots in Qom and this time the police shot and killed nine men and injured scores more. This was followed by demonstrations and shop closings in Isfahan and even Tehran itself. Later that month more riots broke out in Mashhad and seventy-three people were arrested and then nearly beaten to death by the police. The next month riots broke out in Tabriz and the police killed more demonstrators. Businesses, movie theaters, and banks were being burned to the ground there. The situation was so bad in Tabriz that martial law had to be declared and for the first time ever Iranian Army troops had to be deployed in an Iranian city to keep order. In March there were large demonstrations all over Iran against the Shah and the police again fired on the crowds and killed many. In June, the Shah replaced the head of the SAVAK, General Nassiri, with General Moqaddam, who was viewed as being more moderate in dealing with dissenters. The protests in June actually seemed to be more peaceful and the police held their fire, but there still appeared to be no end in sight to the anti-Shah demonstrations.

As late as September 1978, the Defense Intelligence Agency would report that the Shah "is expected to remain actively in power over the next 10 years." Everyone was truly clueless about what was really going on in Iran. No one realized that the end of the Shah's rule was only months away.

By July 1978 I had been in Iran for two years and my assignment there helping the SAVAK build its system for tracking foreigners was wrapping up. The system was operational and being rolled out across the country and seemed to be operating without any major hitches. The daily status meetings had been cut back to weekly status meetings and I now really had almost nothing to do. It was time to go home. I did, however, make one more attempt to meet with the CIA Station at the embassy and again express my concerns about the stability of the Shah's reign and the apparent complete lack of faith in his longevity that was still being expressed by so many of the SAVAK's top officials. I was again politely but firmly blown off by the Station, who now started joking about the paranoid computer geek at the SAVAK. Well, I had done my duty and it was time to go home.

The parting from the Colonel and his family was actually tearful. He gave me a very expensive silver table as a parting gift and said that he and his family would really miss me.

"You must come back to Iran, soon. I will find another job for you at the SAVAK or the Ministry," he said with actual tears in his eyes.

I started to tear up myself. I think the Colonel had taken to thinking of me almost as a son. I was going to miss him too, but I also missed being home.

Alas, I wouldn't be able to ever return to Iran, because just six months later the Shah's government would fall, and he would abdicate and flee the country. A few months after that the Colonel himself would be dead and his family would have to flee Iran for Europe.

At the moment I was about to leave the revolution was imminent, but no one saw it coming. It would change Iran forever, and change my life drastically. I had no idea what was in store for me in the next year, but I would soon find out.

Actually getting out of Tehran proved to be a little difficult. My association with the SAVAK saved me again.

All of my goods had been packed off and I was spending my last night in Tehran at the same Hilton I had resided in when I first arrived. I awoke ready to head for the airport when out my window I saw truckloads of soldiers driving down the street. Just my bad luck – Tehran was about to have its first really violent demonstrations that day. My SAVAK driver and car were nowhere to be seen. No doubt they were now off somewhere trying keep the Shah in power. So, I had the front desk call me a cab. Miraculously, it arrived at the hotel just twenty minutes later.

I hurriedly loaded my suitcases into the cab, jumped in and shouted "Mehrabad", the name of the International Airport. Then I remembered: I hadn't changed all my Rials into US currency. I had a thick wad of the Iranian currency in my pocket and it would be nearly worthless in the US. We were zooming down the unusually empty streets when I spotted a moneychanger's shop. I hollered, "stop", and pointed at the shop. The cab driver screeched to a halt in front of the shop. I jumped out of the cab, and looked up and down the street for:

    a. Demonstrators
    b. Police
    c. Troops

Seeing none, I ran to the shop's door and yanked on the door handle. It was locked! Of course, all the shops would be closed today in support of the demonstrations, whether willingly or not.

I looked through the glass door and saw a man inside. I banged on the door and yelled for him to open it for me. He nodded his head "no". I then had a moment of brilliant inspiration. I took my SAVAK ID card out of my wallet, pressed it up to the glass, banged on the door again, and pointed to the card. Now I was supposed to have turned in my card on my last day at work, but when no one asked for it I just hung onto it. I vaguely thought it might come in handy in making sure I really made it to the airport, and it was now turning out to be invaluable. The man inside immediately got up and opened the door for me. I stepped into his shop, grabbed the big wad of Rial notes from my pocket and shouted: "Dollars!" He nodded no. Damn, he didn't have any US dollars in stock. I then said: "Pound Sterling!" These he had, and quickly exchanged my

Rials for English Pounds. I had no doubt that he wouldn't dare cheat anyone from the SAVAK, so I didn't even bother to count what he gave me. I just dashed back to my waiting cab and the driver practically burned rubber pulling away from the shop and raced down the road to the airport.

I swear I barely breathed again until the British Airways flight to London that I was on board actually took off from the runway and headed away from Tehran. I would change planes in London for an American Airlines flight to Washington, DC and then would be home again after my exciting Middle Eastern adventure.

10

HOME SWEET HOME

The CIA had arranged temporary housing for me until I received all my worldly goods from the international movers. So, I was put up in a furnished apartment in Vienna, Virginia, close by to CIA Headquarters. Little did I realize that I would soon be living in Vienna, Austria.

I was put back to work for the Directorate of Intelligence in my old role of creating software for the analyst workstation. The workstation had evolved considerably since I had left the US and was now running on new hardware. We were even experimenting with advanced graphics processing using an even newer generation of hardware that featured giant cathode ray tube terminals. Somehow it all seemed pretty mundane after being wined and dined, hanging out with big shots, and all the other excitement of living in a foreign country. While in Iran I missed the US, but now that I was home I missed living overseas. My prospects for another overseas assignment were nil, so I just tried to knuckle down and come up to speed again on all the new features of the analyst workstation and the new hardware on which it was running.

While I was slaving away on bits and bytes, many strange and unexpected things were happening in Iran. In January 1979, the Shah suddenly abdicated and fled Iran. Some Ayatollah named Khomeini, who I had never even heard of, was invited by the new government to return from exile in Paris. In February, severe fighting broke out throughout Tehran and Khomeini came into power. A national referendum took place in April and Iran suddenly became an Islamic Republic with Khomeini as its supreme leader.

Everyone, and I mean everyone, at the CIA was completely blindsided by all of this. The White House was suddenly screaming for blood and demanding to know why it hadn't been warned by the CIA about this damned revolution. It wanted to know what kind of knuckleheads were running the CIA.

There was a desperate hunt immediately instigated within the CIA for both scapegoats and any possible saviors. The entire Middle Eastern desk of the Directorate of Intelligence was interviewed and asked if someone, anyone had predicted that the Shah would fall. No one could produce a document that appeared to say anything even close to that. Next, queries were sent out to the CIA Station in Iran with the same question. Pouring through their records they discovered only two reports containing warnings about the Shah's regime being in any way insecure. The source of these two reports was a low-level CIA employee working in a technical role at SAVAK headquarters. His name was Stephen Connor.

"Hip Hip Hooray," the Deputy Director of Intelligence shouted with joy. Not only had someone in the CIA predicted that this would happen, but this person was actually an employee of his own department: the Directorate of Intelligence. So, he could now claim that the analytical arm of the CIA had not been caught by surprise, but had predicted pretty far in advance that the revolution could actually happen.

I was immediately pulled out of my software development role and assigned to work with two of the Directorate's analysts who had the most experience and knowledge of Iran – Larry and Ruby. Our job was to very quickly come up with an analysis of the current Iranian political scene for the White House. We had to emphasize how we weren't surprised by anything that happened and had actually predicted it all ahead of time.

Of course, Larry and Ruby absolutely hated me. They were both academics. Larry taught graduate seminars on the Middle East during the evening at Georgetown University and actually wore a jacket with leather patches on the elbows. Both of them had PhD's and a vast amount of knowledge and expertise about Iran. Here I was, a computer geek who knew nothing about geo-politics, and who had nevertheless somehow made them both look stupid. I was a moron, but a very lucky moron, and they loathed everything about me. I don't think they were sure that I could even write or speak coherently. So, all in all, we made a terrific team for creating a Presidential briefing.

We had a conference room to ourselves and two days in which to produce the briefing. The atmosphere of the conference room veritably crackled with hostility and contempt. Every word Larry and Ruby said to me positively dripped with sarcasm.

"Well, what we need to do is to put together a briefing paper for the Director to present to the President, along with both flip chart and slide-based presentations that will support all of the salient points," said Larry.

Looking at me with an actual sneer on his face, Larry said, "I have no idea what you're going to be able to contribute to the creation of the briefing. We already have copies of the reports you submitted to the Tehran Station. Perhaps you could start off being helpful by getting some coffee for Ruby and me."

I stared right back at him and said, "Perhaps I'll drop by the Deputy Director's office and ask him if he would like some coffee, too." Touché! Larry knew right now I was the Deputy Director's fair-haired boy and at that moment it was likely that I could do no wrong in his eyes. If I let him know that Larry had asked me to get him coffee, a stupendous weight would fall down upon Larry from a great height.

Larry then meekly said, "All right, all right, let's all get started working on this briefing then. Stephen, why don't you start out by telling us everything you know about the revolution and just how you managed to be the only person in the entire US intelligence community to have the slightest inkling that the Shah was in trouble."

With all the petty BS now out of the way, we actually got to work on the briefing. Larry and Ruby managed to put aside their resentments, at least until after we had completed it. By late night the second day we had produced all the material requested for the next day's Presidential briefing. I was really impressed by how much Ruby knew about Khomeini. She had extensive knowledge of all his writings and his theological and political background. Larry had really in-depth knowledge of the history of the Iranian leftist movement and its eventual demise due to some very effective persecution by the SAVAK. I was able to add a little local color and the only real proof we had about anticipating the possible fall of the Shah.

We were all exhausted, but proud of what we had put together. The Director of Central Intelligence (DCI), who was the boss of the whole CIA, and the Deputy Director of Intelligence (DDI), the boss of the Directorate of Intelligence where we worked, would present it to the President the next afternoon at the White House.

The next morning, bright and early, we were in the Deputy Director's office and went over our briefing materials with him and his executive staff. After we had finished our presentation, he said, "Excellent, really excellent. This clearly shows that we were not caught with our pants down over this whole fiasco. I want all of you to come with me to the White House. I don't want to be surprised by anything the President might ask that I'm not going to be able to answer immediately."

Go to the White House? Larry, Ruby, and I looked at each other in astonishment. We were heading to the White House to brief the President, and doing so in just a few hours? I don't know why, but Larry was now looking at me with even more hatred than ever. If he could have caused me to disintegrate by shear mental power, I'd have been turned into dust by his gaze. I would have thought that he would be grateful for the amazing opportunity that had just fallen into our laps, but somehow he now hated me even more than ever. Oh well, I don't care – I'm going to the White House to brief President Jimmy Carter. Woo hoo!

After wrapping up our discussions with the Deputy Director, I swear Ruby spent the entire rest of the day in the ladies rooms working on her hair and makeup. Larry just went back to his cube and sulked. For myself, I immediately became self-conscious about what I was wearing. That day I had worn to work a button down white shirt with very thin blue stripes, a very bright blue tie with whales and dolphins on it (I loved crazy ties in those days), gray slacks, black loafers, and a dark blue blazer. I felt severely under dressed for going to the White House. Why had I picked this day to wear such a crazy tie? I finally tracked down one of the workstation software developers I worked with and swapped my tie for his more conservative dark and light gray striped one. At least I didn't look like a total clown now.

After lunch, we went upstairs to the DCI's office and waited in his secretary's room. Then we all proceeded down to the garage of the building where a mini-motorcade awaited us. There was the DCI's limo where he and the Deputy Director would ride. There were a couple of cars with Directorate of Security personnel in them to provide us with bodyguards. Larry, Ruby, and I rode in the back seat of a station wagon with all our briefing material piled neatly into the back. Both our driver and the man riding next to him were also Directorate of Security bodyguards. Undoubtedly their orders were that in case of any attack they were first to protect the briefing materials and, then if not too inconvenient, to also offer some protection to us as well.

Off we went, down the George Washington Parkway to the Key Bridge, over the bridge to K Street, down K to 17th Street NW, right on 17th to Pennsylvania, and down Pennsylvania to the White House itself. It was a beautiful day and the small crowd gathered in front of the White gawked at us and some of them even took pictures as our motorcade pulled through the gate and onto the White House grounds. Right at that moment I felt like a rock star.

We pulled up to the front of the White House and proceeded to get out of our cars. Larry, Ruby, and I opened the back of our station wagon and unloaded all the briefing materials. A small contingent of the White House press corps took cursory note of us and a few photographers snapped pictures of the entire group entering the White House. Once inside we walked into the West Wing Lobby. The Deputy Director told Larry, Ruby, and me to sit down and wait there. He took the briefing papers from Ruby and handed them to the DCI.

The DDI then said to us, "Wait here with the flip charts and slide show, we'll call you if we need you."

With that, he and the DCI walked out of the Lobby and down the corridor towards the Oval Office. They would wait in the corridor just outside the Oval Office until summoned by the President. We would cool our heels in the West Wing Lobby. It soon occurred to me that all of this might just have been a giant "goat rodeo". We weren't actually going to even see President Carter. We were just there for insurance, just in case the questioning got too intense and the bosses couldn't field what the President was asking. Short of that, we were just going to sit and wait for the entire length of the meeting. That's just what we did.

The Lobby was nice enough. It had large paintings of early American scenes on the walls. There was even a painting of Washington crossing the Delaware. It had three couches, six matching chairs, and three small oval-shaped dark wood coffee tables. The walls were creme colored and the rug brown. It was a lovely room and the three of us sat there in stony silence for an hour. Each of us sat alone on one of the couches not even daring to look at each other. I knew what I would see if I looked at Larry – hatred! He blamed me for this whole ridiculous predicament. I think he would go on blaming me for the rest of his life for any misfortune he might encounter. I had become his arch foe, his scapegoat, and the very bane of his existence. I was genuinely sorry all this had happened to him. I somehow seemed to have single-handedly ruined his entire life. I hadn't intended to do so, it had just happened.

After a little over an hour was up, the DCI and DDI came back to the Lobby. They were grinning from ear to ear. Apparently President Carter, known for being a micro manager and ruthless interrogator of his officials, was in a particularly buoyant mood that day and had thrown them nothing but softballs. He seemed satisfied that the CIA was not being run by complete incompetents. He took their word for the fact that the CIA was all over what was happening in the Iranian revolution and hadn't been surprised by anything that had happened there so far. In other words, they had completely fooled the President.

So, we gathered up all of the supporting materials we had so laboriously crafted over two frantic days and returned to our awaiting mini-motorcade. The small group of White House press at the entrance snapped more photographs. Back to Langley we went. The atmosphere in the station wagon was even gloomier than that in the West Wing Lobby, although it seemed like that would be impossible. We rode back to Langley in total silence. I think we were all disappointed and embarrassed by how excited we had been by the prospect of speaking to the President, and how discouraged we were to find our dreams snatched away for us.

One interesting outcome of this whole fiasco was that a picture of our merry little band appeared deep inside the first section of the Washington Post the next day. The DCI and DDI dominated the picture, and you couldn't see the faces of either Larry or Ruby, but you could clearly see my frowning face at the top left corner of the picture.

Each day the Soviet embassy collected a large number of copies of the Washington Post and eventually sent them back to Moscow in the diplomatic pouch. Of course, some of these copies went to the KGB. Anything appearing in the papers pertaining to the CIA was intently studied and that photograph of us ended up being duplicated, copied, and circulated around KGB headquarters. It eventually came to the desk of one of their Second Chief Directorate Iranian analysts, who glanced at it and then did something of a double-take. There was a familiar face in the upper left hand corner of the photo. He referred to his file of photos of the "enemies of the People" who had been discovered in Iran and quickly found the one he was looking for – the dastardly agent who had smashed vital KGB operations in Iran: Stephen Connor.

Once that analyst reported his findings to his boss, the news quickly rippled through the entire Second Chief Directorate. The mysterious agent in Iran who had caused the KGB so much trouble had now been photographed at the White House. I immediately went from being an annoyance to being a major threat to the Soviets. They now understood that I was not some minor counter-intelligence agent, I was a top-level agent in the CIA who actually had the ear of the President. Overnight, my file at KGB headquarters started to grow exponentially in size. Requests went out to all KGB Residences around the world to spare no effort in finding out any and all information they could regarding this enemy of the State, this dreaded Stephen Connor. I was obviously a major player in the Cold War intelligence battle and the KGB still knew next to nothing about me. That had to change if they were to avoid further embarrassments at my hands. They would go to any lengths to make sure that I caused them no further calamities.

Blissfully unaware of all of the turmoil I was causing the KGB, I found myself in temporary limbo. I had been removed from my software development duties and moved into the unaccustomed role of an intelligence analyst attached to the Iranian desk. Yet, I was completely unqualified to perform this role. I had nothing near the level of knowledge or the academic background possessed by the other intelligence analysts. They were all Ivy League college graduates with at least Master's degrees, and most had PhD's. Larry and Ruby were certainly not going to be willing to work with me, and frankly their vast knowledge of all things pertaining to Iran simply dwarfed the scant bits of information I had picked up after living there for just two years.

I had assumed that after I had participated in creating the Presidential briefing materials I would go right back to designing software. That was not to be. Much to my amazement I had been promoted to a fairly senior level analyst position in the CIA with a pretty hefty salary bump. The DDI didn't want his "analyst who had warned about the fall of the Shah" to be discovered to have just been a computer technician. So, everyone pretended that I was an intelligence analyst on the Iranian desk, but I was given nothing to do.

I was, however, given a small office all by myself in the far corner of the Middle Eastern analytical section of Headquarters. All the other analysts had cubicles, but I got my own office. I had an analyst workstation in my office, and I knew how to use it since I had designed much of the software. Yet I had no actual analytical work to perform. I just showed up every day, went into my office, shut the door and played with the workstation.

I first started subscribing to every Topic I could think of that had anything to do with Iran. I certainly felt obligated to learn everything I could about my reputed area of analytical expertise. Then, since I had so much time on my hands and no real work to perform, I started subscribing to Topics related to the operations of the KGB's First Chief Directorate. There was a tremendously greater amount of information flowing into the CIA regarding the KGB than information related to Iran.

Just for fun, I even subscribed to the Topic of "Viktor Avilov", the KGB man I saw through binoculars during my Iranian ride-along with Jake. I discovered that he had been recalled from Iran after the Revolution, along with most of the other KGB staff. Apparently Moscow was just as unhappy about being surprised by this revolution as was Washington. Viktor's exact current location and activities were unknown at that moment. I also found out that before joining the 8th Department of the First Chief Directorate, he had been a member of the KGB's Directorate S, which was responsible for running "illegal" agents in foreign countries - that is secret agents who covertly enter a country under false identities. Viktor had joined the KGB right out of university and had been with them for well over 20 years. I even ordered up all of the pictures we had of Viktor. I was getting to be a something of a fan of his.

So, I had really taken up a new hobby: learning all I could about the foreign intelligence activities of the KGB. As I've mentioned before, learning had always been a hobby of mine and this new area of research kept me from being bored at work. I read everything I could concerning the KGB. I even ordered background material on the KGB from the extensive archives our reference librarians had compiled. Although I was actually in something like internal exile, I really ended up having a lot of fun. It was like being paid to read real-life spy novels all day.

In May, I was suddenly called into the DDI's office. Well, I figured the fun times were over and that I was going to be sent back to working on software again, but this is not what happened.

I sat down in front of the DDI's huge desk and he said, "Stephen, you know what those maniacs in Iran have done now?"

"No sir," I replied, now becoming completely confused as to where this conversation was going.

"They've issued an arrest warrant for you! Not only that, but they've actually had the balls to request your extradition back to Iran."

"What?", now I was completely confused. "Why?"

"Well, right after these crazies took over Iran they hunted down and killed just about every employee of the SAVAK they could find in the country. We figure they must have murdered over 3,000 of them. After they were done with that, they then started combing through the SAVAK's files looking for information about anyone they deemed to have helped the SAVAK. They seem to have finally come upon a list of all the foreign contractors who were hired by the SAVAK. Arrest warrants have been created for every single one of them and extradition requests have been made to the US, Britain, Australia, and any other countries in which these contractors might now reside. Of course, you must know that the Shah himself is in Mexico right now, and the Iranians are trying to get him extradited, too. Anyway, you were on the list and so there's now an arrest warrant out for you from the Islamic Republic of Iran."

"You had better make sure you stay clear away from the Middle East. I wouldn't want you to ever be on an airplane that even flies anywhere close to Iran. Who knows, it might have some type of mechanical difficulty and the pilot could decide that an Iranian airport was the safest place to divert his plane. We'll be damned before we see you on trial in Iran!"

So, I had become a wanted criminal in Iran.

"Well, anyway I just wanted you to hear this from me personally. Don't worry about it; just make sure to stay away from the Middle East. Carry on the good work!" With that he picked up some papers off his desk and turned his swivel chair so that he was facing away from me – thus dismissing me from his presence.

As soon as I returned to my own office, I immediately cursed myself. I had been so stunned by this unexpected news that I had completely blown an opportunity to ask the DDI to give me some real work to do. I might never get another opportunity to meet with him. I was actually much more upset over this missed opportunity than by my new criminal status.

My internal exile continued unabated. Things were a lot worse for the Shah. In October 1979, President Jimmy Carter very, very reluctantly allowed to Shah to enter the US for medical treatment. What was expected to be a very short visit turned out to be a much longer one due to surgical complications. The Shah's presence in the US completely infuriated the new government in Iran and they immediately demanded that Shah be returned to Iran for a trial and almost certain execution. The US refused, just like they refused to send me back to Iran. I think the Iranians were much more upset over our refusal to turn over the Shah than our refusal to turn me over, though.

So, in November the US Embassy in Tehran was stormed by between 300 and 500 students. The Iranian hostage crisis was starting and wouldn't end until 444 days later in January 1981 after Jimmy Carter left office and the new President Ronald Reagan was sworn in. The Shah would leave the US in December 1979 for a short stay in Panama, and then to a permanent exile in Egypt where he would eventually die of his cancer in July 1980.

Since I had been blindsided by the Iranian arrest warrant and extradition request, I now realized that I was not using my intelligence analyst workstation to its full capabilities. I created a new Topic: "Stephen Connor". I then subscribed to this topic and marked it as "high-interest". This meant that if the Directorate of Intelligence received any intelligence data that contained my name in it, I would know about this immediately. Marking it as "high-interest" meant that as soon it was received on my workstation it would appear on the top of my terminal screen and even be highlighted.

In June 1979, I came to work one morning and saw a highlighted line at the top of my terminal screen. I opened the referenced data and read with amazement that an Ayatollah Saatchi had issued a fatwa calling for the death of all foreigners who had been actively working with the SAVAK. It included my name in the long list of those wicked foreigners. So, I was now on both an arrest list and a list of those condemned to death by an ayatollah. Any Muslim who carried out this death sentence against me would be guaranteed a place in paradise after their death.

Death threats against CIA employees were very rare and are taken very seriously. They were rare because there was an unofficial agreement between the KGB and the CIA to not kill each other's agents. This came about when both sides realized that if they started killing the opposition's agents, then retaliation would be swift and brutal and soon a full-scale vendetta would ensue. So, it was OK to arrest the opposition's agents if they were actually caught in espionage activities, but you couldn't just bump them off no matter how annoying they might be.

As a CIA employee, I was required to immediately report any death threat to the Directorate of Security, my immediate supervisor, and the head of the Directorate in which I worked, i.e., the Directorate of Intelligence. I did exactly that. Boy, did that stir up a quick and dramatic response.

I was immediately called downstairs to the Directorate of Security. There I was interviewed for over an hour in an attempt to gather all of the background information about this death threat and how I happened to be on the list of names contained in this fatwa. Interesting enough, it was soon determined that I was actually the only CIA employee unlucky enough to appear on it. All of the others names seemed to be those of private contractors hired by the SAVAK from the US, Great Britain, and Australia. Apparently, the Iranians had assumed I was just another foreign private contractor working for the SAVAK and were completely unaware of my connection to the CIA.

Next, I was called upstairs to meet again with my dear friend and boss, the Director of Intelligence. I think his affection for me was now cooling a bit. I believe I was starting to become a real pain in his rear end. There were also a couple of members of the Directorate of Security in the meeting.

The Director began, "This is intolerable. We cannot allow these crazies in Iran to get away with death threats against my people." He then turned to the representatives from Security and said, "What are you going to do about this?"

John the tallest, best dressed, and thus likely the most senior of the Security team said: "Sir, we have three options. First, we could assign a security team to act as bodyguards to Mr. Connor. Second, we could provide some specialized training to Mr. Connor. I have already looked up his personnel jacket and found that he had been highly rated in the brief firearms training he had received at The Farm. Third, we can simply brief Mr. Connor on some basic best practices for maintaining personal security, most of which are pretty common sense."

The Director turned to me and said: "Well, I think having a team of bodyguards around you sounds a little over the top to me. What do you think, Mr. Connor?"

"If I'm given the choice, I'd take option number two: some specialized training. I don't need to be a ninja, but I think I'm pretty physically fit and could benefit from some self-defense training and some further training in shooting a handgun. I'm certainly willing to purchase my own handgun if I'm confident that I can shoot it well enough to effectively protect myself."

The Director turned to John and said: "Well, how does that sound to you?"

John thought for a moment and said: "That seems reasonable. We can probably get him sufficiently trained in only a couple of weeks. Do you want us to also equip him with a firearm? Do you want us to arrange the necessary justification for him to be able to carry it concealed on his person?"

The Director immediately said: "Yes to both. Mr. Connor, do you now feel confident that you will be able to protect yourself from any of the nut jobs who may now be gunning for you in order to reserve a place for themselves in paradise?"

I smiled and replied: "Yes sir, I do."

"Then, John, get everything in motion to deal with this matter as quickly as possible."

"We can begin Mr. Connor's training tomorrow, if that's acceptable. As I'm sure you're aware, we have all of the facilities necessary right here at Headquarters."

He then turned to me and said: "Mr. Connor, are you ready to begin tomorrow?"

"I am."

"Then please report to Security first thing tomorrow morning and we will begin your training immediately. Please wear loose, comfortable clothing. We're not going to be able to turn you into an Army Ranger, but we should be able to give you enough information and training to enable you to safeguard yourself in just about any reasonably foreseeable life-threatening situation."

"I look forward to the training, thank you."

So, that's exactly what happened. I reported to Security the next morning in sweats and the training commenced immediately. After two weeks of hard work in learning shooting and self-defense skills my instructors gave me passing grades in shooting a pistol, basic hand and foot strikes, grappling, ground fighting, and some light knife work using training blades. As a graduation gift, I received a Sig Sauer P230, the small .380 ACP semi-automatic pistol that I had shot best during my training. I was fitted out with three holsters for my little Sig – a shoulder holster, leather inside the pocket holder, and a leather belt holster. I was given 250 rounds of ammunition and 4 magazines for the pistol and told that I could get more ammunition anytime I wanted it. I was also encouraged to use the Security pistol range for practice sessions, preferably at least once a month. It was emphasized to me that shooting skills were quite perishable. I was also invited to practice my self-defense skills whenever I wanted, preferably at least four times a year.

After "graduating" from this mini-version of Security training, John presented me with something additional that completely took me by surprise. It was a set of credentials, complete with photo ID and a gold badge identifying me as a special agent for the Department of Defense Special Investigations Section.

I took them, gawked at them, and said: "What's this for?"

John laughed and said: "This will allow you to carry a concealed pistol anywhere in the US. The best way to make sure you never get hassled about carrying a gun is to make you some type of law enforcement officer. The Department of Defense has lots of departments that have armed agents employed within them. The DOD Special Investigations Section is not one of them, though. It is a fictitious organization created by us, with the cooperation of the DOD, in order to allow a very limited number of CIA employees to carry firearms in the US without being questioned. Anyone attempting to contact the DOD SIS will end up being routed right here to Headquarters, where a small staff is always on duty and ready to verify the bona fides of any CIA employee authorized to act as an agent for that organization. With these credentials you will be able carry your handgun anywhere, except here at CIA Headquarters."

He laughed again, and said: "I'm sorry, but this is one of the very few places where you are not allowed to carry your weapon. Only Directorate of Security personnel have that privilege here. So, please leave your pistol in your car when you come to work. In fact, I will arrange for a locking pistol case to be installed in your auto. That's the best thing - to leave it there, while you are at work. Otherwise, in airports, government buildings, just about anywhere else, no one should hassle you about your pistol if you have these credentials with you. In addition, if someone should inquire as to the details of the 'case' you are currently working on as a special agent, you can always say that it's classified and that should deflect any further prying."

All I could say to that was: "Wow!" I was now a federal agent.

While my training had been going on, the Director of Intelligence was contemplating how to best get me out of his hair. During a weekly meeting with his staff, he brought up the topic of Stephen Connor and what to do with him.

"I want to get Stephen Connor out of Headquarters and out of the country as soon as we can. He's sitting on his ass all day here, so he won't be missed. Frankly, if somebody is going to kill him, I want it to happen outside of the US. Where can we send him? Remember, he really doesn't have any real skills other than working with computers. Are there any computer positions open overseas? Anything overseas that doesn't require any particular specialized skills? He's smart, and apparently he can write. He speaks some French. He also speaks some Russian, although I sure as hell don't want to send him there. Any ideas, anyone?"

One of his staff responded: "We did get something of an odd request from someone in the Austrian STAPO through our Station in Vienna. They want us to send them a liaison officer. I'm not even really sure what the liaison officer is expected to do there. Probably just study what the STAPO is doing and see if there is anything we can do to help them out."

The Director said: "That sounds promising. Please refresh my memory - what the heck is the STAPO?"

"It's something of a hybrid organization. It's actually part of the Austrian Federal Police, which itself works under the Ministry of Interior. The STAPO is responsible for counter-intelligence and anti-terrorism activities. It's also responsible for the protection of foreign diplomats and high-level government officials. It even issues passports. Like I said, it's a real hybrid. It's pretty small, with only about 600-700 employees."

"600 to 700 employees? Man, either they are very busy or they do squat," said the Director, laughing.

"Actually, this might be something of a tricky little assignment for whoever gets it. As I'm sure you know, Austria is not a member of NATO and is officially a neutral country. They walk a tightrope between the West and the Soviet bloc. There are over 100,000 Soviet troops just down the road from Vienna. The Soviets and we agree to pretend that Austria is a neutral country, but of course they are really very much of a Western European nation. The Soviets do allow Iron Curtain nationals to freely travel to Austria for shopping, whenever they manage to get their hands on some hard currency. I'm surprised that the Austrians have asked us to provide them with anyone for anything. Whoever goes there will need to practice lots of discretion and keep a very low profile in order not to threaten this sham of neutrality."

"All right, Connor doesn't seem to have gotten into any mischief during his stay in Iran, so I think he can handle this assignment. Sounds to me like there won't be a lot for him to do there except to not rock the boat. Set it up for him to go there as soon as possible. See if we can't make it a three-year assignment. I'd like to not have to think about him anymore for quite some time."

With that, and without any knowledge of the real mischief I had actually gotten into in Iran, my fate was sealed and I would shortly be sent off to Vienna, Austria.

The next month, in August 1979, I was officially informed that I had been promoted again, and would be sent on a three-year assignment to Vienna, Austria. I was given two weeks to get ready to leave. I was told that everyone in Austria spoke English (which wasn't exactly true) and so German language lessons wouldn't be necessary. I was given just two days of briefings on Austria and then told to go home and pack my stuff. There seemed to be a huge rush to get me out of Headquarters. I assumed it was because of the importance of my new assignment. Details regarding exactly what the assignment was were a little vague, but I was assured that all would be clarified once I had arrived in Vienna.

I would be using my DOD SIS law enforcement credentials as my cover. I was going to assist the Austrian Federal Police in some way that seemed very unclear to me – and yes, I would be cleared to carry a firearm in Austria.

11

OFF TO VIENNA

Austria is a very small and quite modern country located in the center of Europe. Its population in 1979 was only about seven and a half million people – about the same as New York City. Austria is about the same size as the state of South Carolina. It is landlocked and in 1979 was bordered by Czechoslovakia, West Germany, Hungary, Yugoslavia, Italy, Switzerland, and Liechtenstein. Vienna was its capital and it had a population of a little over one and a quarter million. Nearly a third of Austria's population lived in the metropolitan area made up of Vienna and its surrounding suburbs.

Vienna was the home of OPEC's headquarters and of a new UNO City – the third major site of UN operations after New York City and Geneva. It was also the spy capitol of Europe. The Russians had only ended their occupation of eastern Austria in 1955. Since Austria was officially neutral, it was just as open to Soviet-bloc travelers as travelers from Western Europe. Vienna was known as "the European city where the KGB felt most at home." Of course, wherever the KGB gathered, you would find US and British spies, too. It was a local joke in Vienna that there were more spies in the city than Austrian troops. Given the small size of the Austrian army, that was likely true. The Austrian STAPO, which had counter-intelligence responsibilities among its many other duties, was notoriously weak, and so rampant spying by all sides went on unabated. Vienna was only thirty miles from the border with the Iron Curtain.

The city itself was truly beautiful – certainly one of the nicest cities in the world. It's located in the northeast of Austria and right on the Danube River. Elevation ranges from about five hundred to fifteen hundred feet. The weather there seemed similar to me to that of the Washington, DC area.

It's definitely a city of culture and art. Home at various times to some of the greatest composers of classical music and to, of course, Johann Straus: the waltz king. In fact, Vienna was still the last great capital of the nineteenth century ball. There were over 400 balls held there each year, almost all of which invariably featured at least some Strauss waltzes. It was filled with theaters, opera houses, museums, and many, many restored palaces. It also hosted a large number of universities. The city was famous for its lovely parks, which make up almost half of the city's area. Last, but not least, were the famous coffee houses of Vienna, where you could not only get an amazing cup of coffee but could easily spend an entire day drinking it while reading the newspaper, discussing politics, or just catching up on local gossip.

In many ways the Viennese seemed trapped in their past glories. Residents still seemed to feel that Vienna was the capitol of the vast and powerful Austro-Hungarian Empire, which had been dissolved at the end of World War I. Most Viennese seemed quite conservative and not at all interested in the world outside of their city. Many times while I was there I would ask for something not usually found in Vienna, like maple syrup, only to be met with amazement that I would want anything so foreign. Everything you could ever want or really need could already be found here, seemed to be their attitude.

Actually, just about all of the food in Vienna really was wonderful. I used to joke when I lived there that it was impossible to get a bad meal in any restaurant in the city, except at the few MacDonald's that were a blight on that beautiful city's culinary scene. Hearty Germanic and Eastern European food was the norm there, with stews, soups, and basic "meat and potatoes" meals most commonly available. The bread and pastries were simply heavenly – and you can't forget the sausages; wonderful staples of many very tasty meals. One of my very favorite meals in this city was "wurst und semmel mit kraut": a simple sausage on a roll with spicy mustard and a side of sauerkraut, all served on a paper plate. They were sold from little food carts stationed on street corners throughout the city for easy access by hungry lunch seekers. Simple food, but absolute taste perfection!

Upon my arrival I checked into the Hilton Hotel by the Stadtpark, a large park in the center of Vienna that contained a famous gilded statue of Johann Strauss. I swear, the CIA must have had a contract with Hilton – no matter where overseas I went I always got booked into one. After checking in, I walked around the area. Apparently there was no crime in Vienna as the Stadtpark was filled with strolling couples, with and without children, throughout the entire night. Try doing that in your city's park. It seemed like this was going to be a very nice place to live for a few years.

The next day, a short walk across the park brought me to the US Embassy. There I checked in with the local CIA Station. This time I wasn't demeaned or ignored or pawned off on the most junior staff member. I walked through the steel doors leading to the secure part of the embassy and was soon ushered into the Station Chief's office. There I was offered coffee and a pastry. The Station Chief warmly greeted me and introduced himself as Martin. His assistant was named Dave. Both of them were dressed in dark slacks, white shirts unbuttoned at the collar, and black ties. They looked to be brothers, although they weren't. I guess they had just been working together for so long that they had started to look like each other.

"Good to have you here, Stephen. Welcome to Vienna. If there is anything we can do to help you during your stay here, please don't hesitate to let me know."

After receiving such a warm welcome, it sounded to me like the Directorate of Intelligence had placed me on the CIA's "don't screw with this guy list". This list was something of an urban legend throughout The Company. Once on it, you had it made. Everyone at the CIA would go out of his or her way to be helpful and red tape would magically vanish for you. It meant that you had a very powerful patron at the top levels of the Agency. I may have been hustled out of Headquarters but I apparently still had a very powerful friend in high places.

"Well, I guess the first order of business is to find out all I can about my assignment with the STAPO. After that, I'll need to find a place to live."

Martin and Dave looked at each other quizzically. Martin then said: "We don't know anything about your assignment. We had assumed that you had been fully briefed about it back home. We're really clueless as to why the STAPO asked for someone from the Agency or what they have in mind for you to do here. We were actually very surprised that they wanted to even associate with the CIA. They pretty much view us as the enemy. They don't want any foreign intelligence agencies working in Austria, but of course they are pretty much powerless to stop all the espionage activities going on here. We were almost as surprised to hear that Headquarters had actually approved their request. All we know is that a Captain Lehner asked for a 'liaison officer' from the CIA to work with him. That's it."

Well this was starting to look ugly right from the start. Headquarters thought the Station would brief me, and the Station thought Headquarters had done it. What the heck was I supposed to do now?

I said, "So, I guess I'm going in cold to my meeting with Captain Lehner?"

Martin shook his head and said rather sadly: "I'm afraid so. You do have some DOD law enforcement cover, don't you?"

"Yes, I'm supposed to be with the DOD Special Investigations Section."

"Well, then I guess I'd just suggest you go there acting all cop-like and see what happens. STAPO is part of the Austrian Federal Police. Hell, apparently they even fight organized crime and guard government buildings. They've got all kinds of stuff piled on their plates. Who knows what they want from you. Lehner knows you are CIA, but I have no idea who else there might also know. I'm really sorry we can't be of more help to you."

"Hey, no problem. I'll let you know what I find out there. What do you need from me? What kind of reporting would you expect from me?"

"Well, you aren't associated with the State Department or the Embassy in any way. You're supposed to be with DOD, not the CIA. Any meetings we may have can just be between two fellow expatriates. Here's my home phone number. I'm sure it's tapped by the STAPO, but there should be no problem with you sometimes calling me and asking me out for a beer. I'd play it by ear for now - just contact me when you learn what the heck is up with STAPO, or sooner if you need my help with anything."

"Now as to housing: one of our consular officers has just left and his apartment is available immediately. I've been there and it's really beautiful, and not too expensive. It's located in Hietzing not far from the Schoenbrunn Palace – which, by the way is a must-see attraction while you're here. I can have one of my girls drive you over right now, if you would like. When are you supposed to have your first meeting with STAPO?"

"Tomorrow morning at 9:30."

"All right, well it sounds like this is a good time to start house hunting, then."

He picked up the phone and called a young woman named Cheryl into his office.

When she arrived, he spoke to her: "Cheryl, this is Stephen Connor. Can you take him over to see Brad's old place?" With that I was off to see what would become my new apartment.

It was a really nice place, but somewhat different from an apartment in the US. It was on the top floor of a four-story apartment house. I'd have to guess that it was built sometime in the 1920's. The elevator was tiny, just about the size of a broom closet, and it was slow as molasses. I usually just took the stairs up to the fourth floor unless I was carrying something heavy or bulky. The apartment itself looked fairly modern inside, and featured European appliances. By European, I mean tiny. The refrigerator and stove looked about the size of units you would find on a boat in the US. The hot water heater was a gas-fired tank-less unit. It was located right in the kitchen wall and the water tubes and burners were visible behind a protective metal grating. When you turned on a hot water tap, you would hear the whoosh of the gas burners going on, followed by the hiss of their flames heating the water running through the tubes. The water got hot very quickly and you had an effectively endless amount available, but this was very different from anything I had experienced before at home or in Iran. I found it oddly fascinating the entire time I lived there.

The view, however, made up for any possible deficiencies this two-bedroom apartment might have. As the "penthouse" apartment, I had a large open patio area just outside the living room with some outdoor furniture and a spectacular view of the surrounding neighborhood. Hietzing was in the western side of the city and bordered the Vienna Woods. Over 70% of this district was devoted to green space – the highest percentage of any district in Vienna. From my patio I could see all of the parkland, the Vienna Woods in the distance, and even part of the grounds of the Schoenbrunn Palace.

The apartment was just off of Hietzinger Haupstrasse, a busy thoroughfare filled with restaurants, coffee houses, shops, as well as some small hotels. The Strassenbahn, or streetcar system, had a route that ran right down this street, making it easy for me to get around Vienna even without using a car. One hotel on this street seemed to attract American tourists who were all attempting to act as the most unattractive, ugly Americans as they possibly could be. This was Vienna: where some of the best food and candy that could be found anywhere in the world was readily available. Yet I was to constantly overhear Americans loudly complaining about such inanities as being unable to find M&M's or Jiffy Peanut Butter. These people made me feel embarrassed to be an American. Why had they come to Vienna when they could have stayed at home and enjoyed all the Jiffy Peanut Butter they wanted?

So, I took over the lease for this apartment and would live there the entire time I was in Vienna. I would reside in it quite happily for three years, although I did have to vacate it temporarily at one point in order for repairs to be made because of extensive damage to its interior. If you continue reading this book, you'll eventually find out how that all occurred.

Early the next morning I got on the U-Bahn (subway) U3 line and got off at the Herrengasse stop. From there it was a short walk to the Ministry of Interior building where Captain Lehner's office was located. The Ministry was located in a Hapsburg palace that had been built in 1811. I would soon discover that many of the government buildings in Vienna were actually old converted palaces. They were all amazing in their interior decoration and every government building I ever went into in Vienna had beautiful pieces of art hung on the walls of the lobbies and hallways. The Ministry of Interior was no different. The building had three stories and the exterior facade was somewhat austere and classical in architecture, but still quite striking. The interior was dimly lit compared to most office buildings in the US. I walked up to the lobby desk and said that I had an appointment with Captain Lehner. I was handed a visitor's badge and directions to Room 276. I walked up the broad staircase leading from the lobby up to the second floor, walked down the hall, and soon came to the door of Room 276. I knocked.

"Kommen Sie, bitte", is what I heard a man's voice say from inside the room. I guessed that meant, "come in", so I opened the door and stepped into the room.

What I saw inside was a fairly small office with a desk and two visitor's chairs. It did have a large window behind the desk, though, with a nice view of the street below. I later found out that the law in Austria stipulated that all offices have windows, and windows that could be opened. What a wonderful law!

The desk was cluttered with huge piles of paper. On the right wall of the office was a large whiteboard, on the left an equally large corkboard. The corkboard was completely covered with photographs, papers, and what looked like fragments of maps. The whiteboard had been almost completely filled with what looked to me like random German phrases, charts, and diagrams - none of which I could decipher.

Behind the desk sat a man. He had the thin build of a long-distance runner. He wore a light gray suit, dark blue shirt, and a very light blue tie. His suit jacket was hung over the back of his chair. This man's features were sharp and his eyes very blue. His hair was blonde and cut quite short. He looked up at me quizzically.

I said: "Captain Lehner?" and reached my hand out in an offer to shake his.

"Ah, Herr Connor! Welcome to my horrid little office," said the Captain, accepting my hand and pumping it enthusiastically. His English was excellent with only the barest hint of a German accent.

"Please, call me Stephen."

"Then you must call me Franz. Please sit and take off your jacket. I can't tell you how happy I am to see you."

"Thanks, it's a real pleasure to meet you as well."

I had gotten into the habit in Iran of starting off any conversation with pleasantries about the weather, family matters, and so forth and was prepared to do that with Franz, but Austrians seemed to like to get to the point much quicker than Iranians.

"Stephen, the very first thing I must ask you is if you brought a firearm to Austria?"

"Yes, I have a pistol," I replied.

"I expected that and the first thing we must do is register it and issue a permit that will allow you to carry the weapon in this country. Did you, perchance, bring it with you today?"

I was actually carrying it in a leather pocket holster inside my pants pocket at that moment, and it was loaded. When I had flown to Vienna I had it unloaded in one of my suitcases and had cleared Austrian customs without them even looking inside them. However, as soon I had arrived at my hotel, I had loaded it and been carrying it with me ever since. I had taken the training I had received from the Directorate of Security to heart and carried my loaded pistol with me whenever it was possible to do so.

Now I realized it had been a serious mistake to do this in Vienna without first checking with Franz. If I had seriously broken the law, how was I going to avoid a possible international incident during my very first meeting with the STAPO? I saw no alternative to just telling him the truth and seeing what happened as a result.

"Yes, I'm carrying it right now."

"Excellent. Can I please see it? I'll need to briefly inspect it and record the serial number."

Well, here goes nothing, I thought. I carefully took my Sig P230 out of my pocket holster, removed the magazine, and cycled the slide to eject the live round out the gun's chamber. I did it in such a way as to gently drop the bullet onto his desk, then locked the slide all the way back so that the pistol was in a completely safe condition, and finally handed it to the Captain.

Franz took it all completely in stride as though nothing out of the ordinary had just happened. He gave the Sig a quick look over and then wrote down the serial number from it. He then picked up his phone and called someone. From the little German I could understand at that moment it sounded like he was asking someone to come into his office. He then hung up the phone and casually reached over his desk to pick up the Sig's magazine and stray cartridge and placed them into one of his desk drawers and closed it. A few moments later, the door to his office opened and a uniformed police officer stepped in. Was I about to be arrested for a firearm's violation?

Franz then gestured up at the police officer and said: "Stephen, this is

Walter. Walter will take this paperwork and will return shortly with a special firearms permit that, as an officially recognized foreign law enforcement representative, will allow you to carry a loaded pistol concealed on your person anywhere in Austria. Walter, this is Stephen Connor, a special agent from the United States who will be observing our ways of working here, and will, I'm sure, be able to offer us invaluable suggestions for improving our efficiency."

Walter shook my hand, and said in a more heavily accented German than Franz's: "Welcome to Vienna. I am very much pleased to meet you."

Franz then picked up my Sig, briefly showed it to Walter, and then said: "This is Herr Connor's pistol, which I have personally inspected. Please take the paperwork and expedite the issuance of the necessary permit. I don't want it to take all day, understood?"

"Ja", said Walter. He then took the paperwork from Franz, turned and swiftly left the office, shutting the door behind him.

Franz then opened his desk drawer and handed me the embarrassing evidence he had picked up from his desk – the single cartridge and loaded magazine from my Sig. He then handed me back my pistol and said, "Please wait until you have the permit before reloading your pistol, if you don't mind."

I felt like I was really blushing, having been caught with my "hand in the cookie jar", so to speak, but all I said was: "Certainly." Then I put the cartridge and magazine in my jacket pocket, and the unloaded pistol back in its holster in my pants pocket.

"Very good – now, let's get to work. I'd like to start off by going over some organization charts of the Austrian Federal Police, and then discussing setting up tours of some of our facilities as well as of the departments located here in the Ministry...."

So it went, on and on and on - organization charts, mission statements, lists of duties performed. Sometime during this very long and dry lecture Walter returned with my permit. It was quite a large document printed on very heavy paper and had lots of stamps and seals on it. Franz told me to just fold it up as best I could and keep it with me whenever I was carrying my pistol. We also took a break for lunch in the cafeteria located in the Ministry and there I first discovered the Austrian love for all things liver. Franz was very excited that liver soup was on the menu that day. It was also then that I discovered my own great personal dislike for liver, but I made a brave show of enjoying my meal.

During the meal, Franz told me quite a bit about himself and his family. He was married with two children. He had a small house located in Penzing, a district to the north of Hietzing. He loved cartoons by Tex Avery and had an extensive collection of the man's Bugs Bunny cartoons. Although Viennese by birth, he had spent most of his childhood in France and was thus viewed somewhat suspiciously by "true Viennese" who had lived in the city all their lives. He was suspected of having been tainted by French thoughts and customs. He suggested that I come to his house someday for a weekend visit where he would share some of his classic cartoon collection with me.

That was actually an unusual request. I soon learned that Austrians do not normally invite anyone to their homes other than family members. They entertain their friends and acquaintances in cafes. Homes are strictly for families. Perhaps Franz truly had been tainted by his time living in France!

Franz sounded to me like he was a very sincere down to earth man with a strange taste for Bugs Bunny. One thing I still didn't know was why the hell he had asked for a CIA liaison officer if all he wanted to do was go over org charts of the Federal Police and arrange tours of police stations. Why lecture me on the Austrian code of justice if he wanted a CIA representative working with him? Had there been some kind of major misunderstanding? Did he really think I was some kind of Federal law enforcement agent?

I didn't know what to do at this point other than just play along and see what happened. I just couldn't think of anything better to do. I remembered what Martin, the CIA station chief, had said about "go there acting all cop-like and see what happens", and figured I should just play out that role and see if anything significant ever developed. About the most I could do was to express a particular interest in the parts of the Federal Police that had a counter-intelligence role; other than that I didn't see that I had much other choice.

After lunch, we returned to Franz's office. He then started a very detailed and lengthy discussion about the differences between the US and Austrian codes of justice. He spent the entire afternoon on this dry as dust topic and it took all my willpower to stay awake and feign some level of interest in it. We did take a brief break in the middle of the afternoon to grab a couple of cups of coffee from the building canteen. During this coffee break, Franz asked: "Do you have family here with you or are you alone?"

"I'm alone."

"May I ask if you're married?"

"I'm not."

"Ah, well you are missing out on one of life's most interesting and perplexing experiences, then. So, are you free tonight?"

Ah, maybe this was finally going somewhere - an after work confidential meeting? I quickly replied: "Yes, I am."

"Very good, then. Are you familiar with the Heurige?"

"No, I'm afraid not."

"Ah, you must accompany me to one tonight, then. They are the epitome of Viennese life. Most Americans think it's our coffee houses, but they shrink in comparison to the importance of the Heurigen to Vienna's life and culture. How can I begin to describe them? I guess you would call them wine taverns that are owned by vineyards. Heurige literally means 'new wine', which is served in all of them. They usually also have simple, but extremely delicious, country food. I would be remiss not to take you to one as soon as possible. Will you come with me to one of my favorite Heurige after work tonight?"

"I would love to do that."

So, the deed was done. Perhaps this is where Franz would finally feel comfortable letting me know the real reason I had been requested to come to Vienna. In the meantime, it was back to his office for a continuation of a monotonous lecture on Austrian law.

Around 6:00 PM we had exhausted this fascinating topic and were both ready to call it a day. We left the Ministry and walked a few blocks to a garage where Franz had his personal car – a small VW. Then it was about a 30-minute drive to the Heurige he was taking me to.

When we arrived, I found it to be a rather homey looking building with simple wooden tables and chairs both inside and out, and lots of customers. We entered and found two seats at a small table in the main room. It was actually quite noisy inside and so I wondered just how effective a setting this might be for any secret conversations that Franz might want to have with me.

A waiter soon appeared and Franz ordered a carafe of "Sturm". When it arrived, I drank some and it was quite pleasant. I wasn't all that big a fan of wine, but this had a very nice light and fruity taste. In short order the carafe was empty and Franz ordered another. He then went over to a sort of buffet counter and came back with food. It was wonderful – ham, potato salad, sausages, cabbage and peppers – all incredibly fresh tasting and delicious.

After eating a bit of this tasty food, I suddenly realized that I seemed to be very drunk. What I didn't know at that time was that Sturm was a notorious drink in Austria. It was actually a type of fermented grape juice that was very easy to drink but had a kick like a mule. It had a high alcohol content and would get a novice Sturm drinker extraordinarily drunk in a very short time. I soon felt like the room was about to start spinning and began to doubt whether I would be able to stand up or not. The noise of the place seemed deafening and soon all I wanted was to find out from Franz where the men's room was located. He pointed the way and I literally staggered to it. I vomited into a toilet there to the great amusement of the other occupants. I then cleaned off my face and staggered back to our table. Franz seemed none the worse from the Sturm and I tried to remember how much of it I had seen him actually drink.

Franz looked concerned and said: "Are you feeling all right?"

"I'm drunk," I slurred.

"Nonsense, I think the food here has disagreed with you. Let me get you some bread, it will settle your stomach." With that he got up, went over to the buffet counter, and came back with a loaf of dark bread. He cut a slice and handed it to me.

"Eat this, it will settle your stomach. You can't be drunk, this Sturm is just fortified grape juice – mild as mother's milk," he lied.

If I hadn't been so drunk I would probably has seen right through his lie, but I was well beyond that. The bread did help my stomach, though, and I felt a little better. Franz offered me another glass of Sturm and told me to sip it and alternate sips of Sturm with bites of the bread. Yes, he was really looking after me, all right. Anymore looking after me like that and I would soon be passing out.

Then he said: "Well, Stephen, I have really been monopolizing our conversations today. Please, tell me all about yourself."

Then the interrogation began in the most friendly and nonchalant manner that Franz could manage. It was an interrogation, nevertheless.

"So, Stephen, where were you born?"

"San Francisco."

"Ah, yes, that's where the crookedest street in the world is located. What's the name of that street, I can't remember?"

So, he was trying to ascertain if I really knew San Francisco well.

"Lombard."

"Ah yes, Lombard Street, that's it. So, how large is the Special Investigations Section?"

Now was the time for me to pull my wits together and remember my cover story. I replied, "We have 60 special agents and about 250 employees in total."

"What kind of cases do you work on there?"

"I'm afraid they are really all classified or confidential."

"Oh, I'm sorry, I'm not trying to pry. Where did you train?"

"At Quantico."

So it went, pleasant and apparently no-pressure questions that went on and on. I now realized that Franz had definitely gotten me drunk in order to question me. I didn't know why he had done that, but it was really happening to me. I asked for some coffee and Franz got up and shortly returned with a very small cup of fairly weak coffee. Then the questions continued.

"It's interesting to see that you carry a German-made pistol. All of the US law enforcement agents I've encountered carry American-made revolvers. How did you manage to end up with a Sig?"

"We're a special investigative agency and we have wide leeway in selecting our personal firearms. The Sig is just the handgun I shoot the best."

On and on the questions came. I clearly felt like I was holding my own, and suddenly the thought came to me that I had no idea who this man really was. Someone I had never met before had directed me to his office. Even if it was Captain Lehner's office, I had no way of knowing if this was the real Captain Lehner. Maybe that's why he wasn't able to tell me why I had been summoned to Vienna. Maybe this man actually didn't know why I was here.

Then the thought struck me that my pistol was unloaded in my pants pocket, with its magazine and the extra round for the chamber in my jacket pocket. I told Franz, or whomever he was, that I was going to go to the men's room again. I grabbed my jacket off the back of my chair, went into a bathroom stall and with great difficulty reloaded my Sig P230 and reholstered it in my pocket holster. If I were so drunk that I could barely reload my pistol, I wondered how well I would do if I actually had to shoot it. Regardless, it was time to find out what was planned for the rest of the evening. I returned to our table, where my companion smiled at me most amiably.

"Franz, I'm afraid I am feeling unwell. Could you please take me back to my hotel?"

"Why certainly, Stephen, perhaps you are being affected by jet-lag."

I then inquired: "How much do I owe for my drinks and food?"

"Nothing, absolutely nothing. You are my guest tonight."

With that, we left and I very unsteadily walked to Franz's car. I got in and wondered where he was really going to take me. I slumped into my seat and closed my eyes, feigning sleep, but kept my hand right by the pocket containing my pistol. Franz started the car and we drove off. I occasionally opened my eyes the tiniest bit to snatch a glimpse of where we were driving, but I knew so little about Vienna at this point that I really had no idea of where we were going. In about a half-hour, though, things started to look familiar, and sure enough shortly thereafter we were in front of the Hilton. Franz got out, opened my door and helped me out. A doorman rushed over to us, but Franz reached into his pocket, showed the doorman his police ID, and gestured him away from us.

"Stephen, my friend, do you have your room key?"

"Yes," I replied weakly. I was really starting to feel very badly again.

"Please, give me your key," said Franz.

I did as instructed and decided to try and act even more drunk and helpless than I really was.

Then Franz walked me to the elevator, up to my room, and laid me down on the top of my bed. He took off my shoes and placed my room key on the nightstand next to the bed. He then said, "Stephen, please don't feel obligated to come into my office tomorrow. I fear you are suffering badly from jet lag and could use a day of rest. Why don't we meet again the day after tomorrow at 9:30? I will see you then. Good night and Servus (good bye)."

With that he left the room, shutting the door behind himself. I lay still for a few minutes listening intently for any strange sound. Then I sat up and turned on the light. Everything looked normal and I appeared to be completely unharmed. What was going on? I didn't know if I was relieved or disappointed. Why all this drama of getting me drunk? Oh well, hopefully I would figure it all out tomorrow. Right now, I just wanted to sleep, and so I undressed and immediately went to bed.

12

THE TRUTH FINALLY REVEALED

I woke up the next morning with a terrible sick hangover. I was incredibly grateful that I didn't have to see Franz that day. I was in no mood to be toyed with by him again. I ordered room service, including three large bottles of sparkling water and two orders of toast and preserves. I drank two bottles in short order and ate one order of the toast with a very light coating of butter and preserves. That seemed to satisfy my incredible thirst and settle my upset stomach, so I just went back to sleep to avoid the terrible pounding headache. I woke up again just before noon. I felt somewhat human now, so I showered and dressed. I drank the last bottle of water and had some of the remaining toast and headed out for the embassy. I needed to speak with Martin, if he was available, about all of the strange goings-on with Franz. I also wanted to know if Martin had a picture of Captain Lehner so I could find out if I was dealing with him or an impostor. All kinds of crazy ideas about various possible conspiracies were whirling through my head.

At the embassy, Martin was available and actually seemed happy to see me. I clued him in on my first day's experiences with Captain Lehner.

"Phew! Sounds like you had a very interesting time with him. I'd guess that he doesn't want to get to the point of your visit until he really trusts you. I'm afraid the Austrians have a long tradition of getting people drunk in Heurigen to take advantage of them. The often told story of why the Russians suddenly left Austria in 1955 is that they got the commanding general of the Soviet occupation forces drunk in a Heurige and then got him to sign the order for the troops to leave immediately. The next morning he was supposedly too embarrassed to admit what had happened to him, and so the Soviets actually withdrew. Wonderful story – it might even be true."

"Do you have a picture of Captain Lehner?"

"Sure, hang on a minute, I'm sure I have one in my desk...Ah, yes, here's the Captain."

With that he held up a picture of the man with whom I'd spent most of the previous day, this time in a police uniform, but definitely the same man. Well, so much for that great theory!

"Yeah, that's him," I said.

"Well, then, I guess it just was all a test. I think you're going to have to simply play along and wait to see when he actually trusts you enough to get to the real point of why he asked you to come here. Who knows how long that's going to take?"

"Great," I muttered. "Oh well, I guess I can try to keep it up until my liver blows out."

Martin laughed heartily at my predicament, and I couldn't blame him.

"Well, how about some lunch, then? There's a great little cafe just around the corner. You up for a meal?"

"Yes, I think I am. Actually all of a sudden I'm quite hungry. Just no wine with lunch, OK?"

We both laughed, and then grabbed our jackets and headed out to lunch. After that I went for a walk in the Stadtpark. I had dinner by myself in a restaurant near the hotel. Tomorrow I would face Franz again. I wondered what he had up his sleeve for me next?

Well, on that day and for the next few months, all he had for me were tours led by junior officers of Federal Police facilities. Tours of Federal Police stations around the country. Tours of communications centers. A tour of their data center. A tour of the Federal Police Aviation Unit. Tours of their canine units. Ride-alongs with highway patrol units.

I also learned that there were really two police forces in Austria: the Federal Police, which primarily had authority in the urban areas of Austria, and the Gendarmerie, who policed the rural areas of the country. I visited the headquarters of the GEK, the anti-terrorist and hostage rescue unit of the Gendarmerie. They put on a special training exercise just for me and I was amazed at how well they performed. I then had more tours of other Gendarmerie facilities. I was also informed that there were a total of over 900 Federal Police and Gendarmerie police stations in Austria, and I feared that I would end up visiting every single one of them before I found out why I had been brought to Austria.

One day, Franz suddenly arranged a tour of one of the nine Federal Police training facilities. This one was in Lower Austria, the state in which Vienna was located, and he hosted this visit himself. It took two years to train an officer up to the standards required by the Federal Police. We spent the entire day there and at the end of the day I found myself at the pistol range. Franz insisted that we have a shooting contest between just the two of us. My Sig P230 against his Walther PPK. Much to his surprise, I beat him - and I mean he really seemed surprised. I think this was another one of his tests for me and I guessed that I had passed it.

After our contest, Franz said, "Stephen, could you come to my home this Saturday afternoon? I want you to meet my wife and children and spend the afternoon and evening with us. My wife is an extraordinary cook and I don't think you will be disappointed. I'm also anxious to show you some of my collection of Tex Avery films (oh yeah, the Bugs Bunny cartoons). Did you know that the French view Tex Avery as one of the true geniuses of film making?"

"No, I didn't realize that, and yes, I would be very honored to be a guest at your home. What can I bring?"

"Please, Stephen, just bring yourself."

I made a mental note to at least bring a bouquet of flowers for Franz's wife. I was not showing up empty-handed.

Early in this period of taking tours of Federal Police facilities, my furniture and other worldly goods had finally arrived in Vienna and I moved into my apartment. Every evening after work I spent a little more time getting my home organized. I also learned where to shop in my neighborhood and began to get to know my neighbors in the building. All of them were very polite and correct, but not very friendly. I soon found out that this was a really common behavior among Viennese. They weren't anything like the Iranians I had experienced. They were much cooler and nowhere near as open or generous.

So, Saturday had finally come and I drove to Franz's house in my new VW Golf – the car that was known as the VW Rabbit in the US. It was a used car I picked up through the Embassy. Another staff member was heading home and needed to sell it, and so I got what I thought was a pretty good deal on this little car. Armed with his driving directions I soon made it up to Penzing and found Franz's house.

Like most Austrian houses it was quite small. Real estate was much more expensive than in the US and most Viennese lived in apartments. Franz was really fortunate to have a detached house for his family. I stepped out of the car with my very large bouquet of flowers and knocked on his door. Franz opened, laughed, and said, "Stephen, I told you not to bring anything. Now you will spoil my wife."

He then shouted, "Lena!"

His wife appeared wearing an apron and fussing with her hair. I had expected a blonde-haired blue-eyed woman to match Franz's look, but instead I saw before me a very short dark haired woman with a relatively dark complexion. She looked more Eastern European than Germanic.

Under her apron she wore a bright blue dress with a flower design on it. Two children soon appeared in the foyer: Christine and Albert. Both looked more like their mother than their father and were very well dressed and extremely polite. Christine was twelve and Albert was ten. After brief introductions they both vanished into the children's part of the house. In Austria, children are to be seen and not heard.

After Lena had thanked me profusely for her flowers, she was off to the kitchen and Franz led me into his private study. It was a small room with windows looking out onto the very small backyard of the house. The room had a desk and chair, a small couch, and a television and VCR that were set on a chrome and glass stand. Under the stand was a neatly stacked and very large collection of VCR tapes.

Franz offered me a drink, and I asked for an apple juice. He laughed, and said he promised not to serve me any Sturm today and wouldn't I really prefer a beer? I agreed and he quickly returned with a mug of excellent Austrian beer.

He then said: "Now, I've been dying to show you my video collection. Let's start off with one of my favorites. It was an Academy Award-winner: 'Nighty Night Bugs'." Thus began our own private Bugs Bunny film festival. He gestured for me to sit on the couch and loaded up the VCR. He turned up the volume on the TV fairly loud, and sat down next to me. When the cartoon started, he turned to me and suddenly said, "Stephen, I need your help."

"How can I help you?"

"Stephen, I'm afraid, but I have to trust someone. I believe that the KGB has penetrated the STAPO and I don't know anymore who is loyal and who is a traitor. That's why I have asked for help from the CIA. I need you to help me find out who is working for the KGB. I can't use my own staff because I don't know whom to trust anymore. Can you help me?"

Well, this was a task way, way over the head of a software developer. What Franz needed was someone from the Directorate of Operations who specialized in counter-intelligence. Alas, all he had right now was me. What possible help could I be to him?

So, even though I was full of doubt I nevertheless blurted out: "Of course I will." Well, I had really done it this time. I had committed the CIA to help a neutral nation's counter-intelligence officer root out Communist infiltration of his own department. What other choice did I really have, though?

Franz, then stood up, reached under the couch cushion on which he had been sitting, and pulled out a file folder. He sat again, opened it, and to my utter astonishment, right on top of the pile of documents it contained was a picture of my old friend, Viktor Avilov!

I blurted out, "I know that man, and his name is Viktor Avilov. Is he here in Austria?"

Franz looked both a little shaken and astonished at the same time. He said, "Yes, he is. I took this picture a few weeks ago. I believe he's now working out of the Russian Embassy here in Vienna."

"But that makes no sense," I said. "He works in the 8th Department of the KGB's First Chief Directorate. They are responsible for Turkey, Iran, and Afghanistan. What is he doing in Vienna?"

As soon as I said that, I regretted it. I had just shared some very classified information with a non-US citizen. That information had definitely been classified by the CIA as NOFORN - that is, not to be revealed to foreign nationals. Yet, I had just done that very thing. I needed to cool down and deal with this situation with a lot more care and thought, and stop blurting out whatever occurred to me!

Franz stared at me with his mouth wide open, and with a look of total astonishment on his face. I think his respect for me just went off the charts. Here was a man siting right next to him who appeared to know every KGB agent in the world by sight and where they worked. Suddenly, the look of surprise actually turned into a look of fear. He was probably wondering just what he had gotten himself into.

He took a chug from his beer and gathered his wits. I guess he figured that he had already gone too far to pull back now, so he plunged ahead with his story.

"A few years ago I noticed a very interesting fact about the STAPO: we seemed quite effective in watching over the operations of the US CIA, the West German BND, and the British MI-6 in Austria, but were very ineffective when it came to the KGB. From my experience and training, I had formed the opinion that the KGB was actually a far less effective intelligence organization than the other three. Yet, we seemed to know nothing about their operations in Austria. How could this be? What was the KGB doing that was preventing us from keeping their operations under effective surveillance?"

"A short time later, I happened to attend an all-day conference for all the top officers in the STAPO. In some conversations between our formal sessions, I mentioned this fact to quite a few of my fellow attendees. I probably spoke loudly enough for even more officers to have heard what I was saying, as I was feeling pretty angry about this fact. How could we be so ineffective against the Soviets?"

"Then, just one month later we caught a low-level KGB officer trying to recruit a diplomat from the Foreign Ministry. How interesting, I thought, just a month after loudly complaining about how ineffective we were against the KGB, we suddenly catch them red-handed in a very clumsy operation. Of course, the Russian had diplomatic immunity and all we could do was expel him from the country. I also heard that he had been scheduled to return home shortly, anyway. His expulsion really wasn't any real loss to the KGB."

"Then I asked myself: coincidence or conspiracy? Had the top level of the STAPO been penetrated by the KGB? If so, how could I find out for sure without tipping anyone off?"

"So, over the last few years I've been collecting information on every odd thing that seems to have happened in STAPO in connection with the KGB. I haven't been able to find anything concrete that points the finger at anyone in particular, but I've come up with a collection of oddities, as you can see for yourself."

"The photograph you just saw was only the latest one of these. You see, only you and I seem to know that this man is a KGB agent. There is no file on him in STAPO, yet I myself took this picture of him. I saw him completely by accident on two occasions. The first time was when I was speaking with a surveillance team member outside of the Soviet Embassy. I just happened to glance up and saw him leave the building. For some reason, something seemed wrong about the man and so his face stuck in my mind. The very next day, I saw the same man again walking out of a cafe near my office. I managed to take his picture without being noticed. After developing the film myself, I went though our files. There was nothing about him; he doesn't exist as far as STAPO is concerned. Now you confirm that he is a KGB agent. How can we have nothing on file about him? We are supposed to have files on all of the Soviet Embassy staff. Where is his file?"

That was quite a story. Franz was certainly in a sticky situation. One of his colleagues, or even one of his bosses, might be an active KGB agent and would certainly stop at nothing to prevent being discovered. How would anyone be able to find out who it was, or if they really existed at all? Maybe the STAPO was just unlucky or mistake-prone – but that seemed pretty unlikely. Franz seemed pretty smart and down to earth and I found myself believing his story. Now what to do about it?

So, I said to Franz, "OK, the first thing I need to do is to ask the local CIA Station for help with this. They should be very interested in hearing all about what you've discovered and I'm pretty sure I can get some of their resources made available to us to help get to the bottom of this. Is that OK with you?"

"I don't know. The more people who know about this, the more likely it is to get out. I'm going to be in enough trouble if anyone finds out I've been talking to you about this. If they find out that the whole CIA is in on it, I'm sunk!"

"That's true, but what alternative do we have?"

"Please, Stephen, before you broadcast this all over your Embassy, can't we just try and find out some more information on our own? I've been hamstrung because of my current workload and the fact that I'm sure I'm being carefully watched by whoever has penetrated STAPO. I made myself very noticeable when I first made my complaint at the conference. You, however, would have much more freedom to pry. You are just a visiting US law-enforcement officer studying our methods. I've gone to great pains to make sure that's what everyone at STAPO thinks. You have nearly complete freedom to go about and poke into our operations. Couldn't you do just that? Can't we start off by keeping a very low profile in this investigation?"

I thought about what he had said and I had to agree with Franz. It couldn't hurt anything for me to just poke around a little before broadcasting to the entire CIA and US Embassy about what he feared. It would help strengthen the case when we finally decided to press for a bigger investigation if we could put together more evidence. My big advantage was that the KGB likely knew nothing about me. I was a real nobody in the CIA and so chances were that anything I did would hardly attract any of their attention. At least, that's what I thought!

"OK," I said. "Where do I start, then?"

Franz sounded relieved and even excited by my response and said, "So far I've kept you away from our STAPO operations. I think it's time you started visiting them and seeing whatever you can of our operations in this area. I'd like you to be introduced to all the key personnel and perhaps even have you observe some of our surveillance activities first-hand. Then we can get together and see if you have noticed anything out of the ordinary. I'm hoping that the fresh eyes of an outsider will see something that I'm missing. What do you say?"

"I say OK, let's do it!"

"Stephen, I can't begin to tell you how much this means to me. I feel better than I have for years. I think we are going to finally find out what's really happening inside STAPO. Thank you so much!" He actually hugged me, he was so excited, and that was a very un-Austrian thing to do.

"On Monday I will begin arranging your tours of STAPO. I'll have you escorted by a junior officer, as I've done in the past. I don't want to attract any further attention to myself. I think my office may even be bugged. Maybe my home is, too. Yes, this is all going to work out so well! Now, let's get back to actually watching some more of these wonderful Tex Avery films."

With that, everything suddenly popped back to normal again. We drank a little beer and watched cartoons. At dinnertime, we went into the dining room and Lena served us a wonderful meal. We started with a delicious homemade tomato soup. This was followed by an amazing Austrian goulash, much richer and heartier than the Hungarian version of this dish, some dumplings, and a salad with sour cream dressing. I didn't think I would have any room for dessert, but when I saw and smelled Lena's amazing apple strudel, I suddenly found room for quite a bit of it. I ended up completely stuffed but enjoyed every bite.

After dinner we retired to the living room and drank coffee and talked and laughed. Franz looked about 10 years younger to me and I think his wife definitely noticed that there was something different about him. We ended the evening with Franz trying to teach me how to sing some classic Austrian drinking songs. It was hilarious! Afterwards, I finally headed back to my apartment. Monday was going to be a very interesting day for me.

Not being a complete fool, I decided the next day to call Martin at his home and ask him if he would like to go out for a drink. He agreed to meet me at the Schweizerhaus, which was located about halfway between our homes, for a few beers. When I arrived, he was already there at a back corner table drinking a beer, and he had another one on the table waiting for me.

He asked as I sat down: "What's up?"

So, I told him all the details of my visit with Franz at his home the previous day. Martin gave a low whistle and said: "Now there's a real can of worms."

I said: "Please keep this under your hat for the moment. Franz is very concerned about his story leaking out and he'd have a fit if he knew I was even telling you about it. I just thought it was too risky not to let anyone at The Company know why I was really asked to come here."

"Good move on your part. Yes, I'll keep this all on the QT for now. Frankly, I don't know what more we could do about it anyway. With Austria's declared neutrality, and their extreme sensitivity about never being seen to favor either side in the Cold War, I'm not sure if the CIA would want to ever get involved in poking around inside their counter-intelligence organization. I can't begin to imagine the diplomatic shit-storm it would cause if something like that were discovered. I definitely think you are on your own on this one, at least for the time being. Hell, if I reported this back to Langley, I have a feeling you would be on the next plane home. So for now, mums the word."

I felt immensely better now that I had done at least something to cover my ass. I had done my duty and reported on my activities to a senior CIA officer. I couldn't be accused of going totally rogue on this operation. Also, the more I thought about it the more I felt there was very little for me to be concerned about, anyway. All I was going to do was to continue doing what my cover story required me to do – study the operations of the Austrian Federal Police. STAPO was an important part of that organization, so of course I would want to spend some time studying it to whatever depth the Austrians felt comfortable allowing me. Really, what bad could possibly come from this?

Martin finished his beer, and said: "Well, I've got to run – lots to do with the family today. Good luck Stephen, and be sure to let me know if anything significant comes from your poking around in STAPO's business."

With that he left, waving to me as he stepped out of the door. I finished my beer, paid up, and left shortly after him.

On Monday I showed up in Franz's office as usual. He looked absolutely full of joy and greeted me with a huge smile. "My friend Stephen, how are you this fine morning? Lena wanted me to tell you how much she enjoyed your company on Saturday, and how much she loved your flowers. I sincerely hope you enjoyed yourself as much as we did."

"Absolutely, I had a wonderful time there. You were right; your wife is a wonderful cook. I can't remember when I've ever had such a great meal."

"You must come again, some time soon. Now, I've arranged your schedule for this week. You'll be speaking with some of the staff of STAPO, the counter-intelligence function of the Federal Police in which I play a small role. It has required a bit of delicacy on my part to set up your meetings, as I'm sure you must realize. This part of the Federal Police deals with many matters that the Austrian government feels are highly confidential. So, if you find some of the people you speak with somewhat less than completely forthcoming, please do not take personal offense."

"I understand completely and greatly appreciate this opportunity to study your operations at any level which you deem appropriate." Our whole conversation was pretty restrained just in case Franz was right about his office being bugged.

"Excellent, Lieutenant Bauer will be your guide through our STAPO maze. Feel free to ask him any questions you may have and I guarantee that he will answer all that he is able to. He should be here in about a half hour, in the meantime would you like to join me in the canteen for a cup of coffee?"

"I would, thank you," and with that we enjoyed a cup of coffee, some very light conversation, and returned to his office thirty minutes later. There Lieutenant Bauer joined us a few minutes later.

Bauer was a large physical specimen, indeed. At least six feet four inches tall, he was extremely muscular in appearance. He looked like he regularly lifted weights. He had blonde hair worn in a crew cut and green eyes. He wore a Federal Police uniform and he looked very striking in it. When introduced to me, he vigorously shook my hand with an extremely firm grip, just short of being painful to me. Franz introduced him to me as David.

"Stephen, David here will be your guide today, and probably for at least the next week. I would love to convey you about STAPO myself, but I'm swamped with administrative duties right now. Nevertheless, I'm sure David will do just as good a job as I can."

He turned to Lieutenant Bauer and said: "David, are you ready to start the tour?"

"Yes, Captain."

"Then please start it right now, Lieutenant."

David first took me upstairs to the third floor of the Ministry building to meet with Dr. Dorn, who was the head of STAPO. The third floor of the Ministry building was even more luxurious than the second floor where Franz had his office. The ceilings were higher, there were both paintings on the walls and sculptures in the hallways, and all the offices had outer rooms for secretaries. The most senior officials of the Ministry of Interior and the Federal Police occupied these offices. So, it looked like Dr. Dorn was something of a heavyweight in the Austrian government.

Lieutenant Bauer and I waited in an outer room that served as the office for Dr. Dorn's secretary. His secretary was a uniformed male STAPO officer who kept a very close eye on me the entire time. His name was Nico, and in his favor he did offer me a coffee to drink while we waited. Nevertheless, Nico gave me an unsettled feeling. Maybe it was because of the intensity with which he stared at me with his brilliantly blue eyes. Somehow his eyes looked artificial to me. They looked like doll's eyes. After about fifteen minutes of waiting Dr. Dorn finally summoned us into his office.

His office was amazing, more like that of some kind of imperial ruler than that of a government civil servant. The walls had a covering that looked like blue velvet. A massive chandelier hung from an ornate painted ceiling that featured figures of Austrian nobility in hunting scenes. All of the furniture in the office, including the desk, was massive in size and made of some kind of beautiful dark wood with elegant carvings. Dr. Dorn stood and gestured me into one of the very ornate chairs sitting in front of his desk. The chair looked like it belonged in a museum and I actually felt a little guilty sitting on it.

"Herr Connor, welcome to my office. I hear that Captain Lehner has been keeping you very busy inspecting many of our Federal Police facilities and that you now would like to study STAPO. I must say that I'm honored that the United States Department of Defense considers our very small police force worthy enough of its time to study. I'm also somewhat surprised that they would have any interest in our organization at all. What brought us to your attention?"

Well, he was immediately putting me on the spot. He was asking me what the hell I was doing here.

"We are very interested in all of the law-enforcement organizations operating in Europe. Since my agency often deals with classified investigations and surveillance operations, we are also interested in finding out how some of the better-run security services are performing their duties. The US has had a long tradition of sharing knowledge of best law-enforcement and security practices with other nations, and now I think we have come to the realize that we have just as much to learn from other countries as we have to give to them. We have stopped assuming that we know best about all aspects of security. I must admit that our current understanding of STAPO's operations is quite limited, but what we do know is that you are doing an excellent job in spite of very limited resources. So, it seems like yours is an organization from which we could learn a tremendous amount. The Department of Defense is very grateful for any aid which you could give us and is also more than willing to assist you in any way that might be practical, given your country's firm commitment to maintaining its neutrality."

Dr. Dorn stared silently at me for what seemed like a very long time, and appeared to be considering at length what I had just said to him. I had a feeling that he was either going to tell me to hit the road or just come up with some way to appease me that would result in my learning the absolute minimal amount of information possible about STAPO. Anyway, I had answered him in such a way as to avoid the entire question of who initiated my visit – Franz or the DOD. I wasn't sure exactly how Franz may have explained the reason for my coming to Vienna and wanted to avoid that whole topic, if possible. So, I just waited and met his stare.

"Alright, Herr Connor. I think I understand the reasons for your visit to us a little better now. However, I must tell you in all honesty that there is really very little about STAPO's operations that we can share with you. We will do all we can, but I'm afraid that will be quite limited, because of our concerns for the security of our nation. The United States is neither an ally nor an enemy to us, but you are a foreign nation. All nations have secrets, which they wish to keep from other nations in order to remain secure and independent. You have them, and so do we. Do you understand what I am telling you?"

"Yes, I do. I understand completely."

"Very good, then. We have no wish to offend either you or the nation you represent, so I probably have made this all much more complicated than really necessary. I just wanted to make myself perfectly clear. If you will kindly step outside into my secretary's office and send Lieutenant Bauer in, I would like to have a brief conversation with him regarding your tour of STAPO. Would that be alright with you?"

"Certainly," and I did exactly as told. I ended up sitting in Dr. Dorn's secretarial office for about fifteen more minutes with the doll-eyed Nico, until Lieutenant Bauer finally came out and led me to the first stop of our tour.

My tour of STAPO that week ended up being something of a complete waste of time as far as gathering any information on possible moles within the organization. I toured their central file facility, but wasn't able to actually see the contents of any of the documents. I toured the department of STAPO that dealt with fighting organized crime and was given free reign to speak to any of the staff, but this wasn't getting me anywhere. I also toured the department concerned with guarding government buildings and spoke with many very pleasant people there. I visited the Passport Office where friendly STAPO officers told me all the exciting details of the passport issuance process and how foreigners were officially registered. They even showed me my own registration record. Finally, the week was wrapped up with a tour of their personal protection unit, which was responsible for providing bodyguards for top government officials and visiting foreign dignitaries.

One important result of my visit that I was completely unaware of was that the KGB now knew of my presence in Vienna. This caused a huge ripple of excitement and concern through the local KGB Residence and all the way back to Moscow. Here was the dreaded Stephen Connor again. He was now poking around in another counter-intelligence organization that the KGB had penetrated. Not only that, but this capitalist thug had arrived in Vienna just at the very moment when the KGB was planning to initiate a major operation against the US Embassy there.

That was why Viktor Avilov had been sent to Vienna – not because of his experience in working with the 8th Department on Turkey, Iran, and Afghanistan, but because of his prior experience in working in Directorate S running illegal agents in foreign countries. He was now running an illegal agent with the cover name of Harri Aalto. Harri was traveling on a Finnish passport and was now living in the Marc Aurel Hotel right in the heart of Vienna. Harri's job, in turn, would be to run a KGB agent who was an American diplomat. This diplomat was being transferred by the State Department to the Embassy in Vienna in just a few months. When he arrived, Harri would take over as his control. My sudden appearance in Vienna could not be a coincidence. The only question the KGB had was whether I was there to unmask their STAPO penetration, defeat their Embassy operation, or both. I had just given the KGB a major, major headache!

Of course, in my ignorance I had no idea that any of this was happening. Mark Twain once said that in order to be really successful in life you had to have two things: ignorance and self-confidence. At that moment I certainly had both, but my prospects for success were actually starting to look very doubtful.

So, at the end of my week of touring all of the truly unimportant parts of STAPO, I was back in Franz's office. He said: "Let's step out for some coffee, shall we?"

"Sounds like a great idea. I could use the fresh air and a little walk. Why don't you take me somewhere we haven't been before."

As soon as we were outside the building, I briefed Franz on my complete lack of progress discovering any useful information about the mole or moles in STAPO. He looked pretty crestfallen after I finished.

He said, "That sounds very discouraging, where do we go from here?"

"I'm not sure, perhaps we can go over your file some weekend and maybe I'll see something that you missed. As for right now, I'm stymied. I've seen everything in STAPO that I'm going to be allowed to see and I'm no further in finding a mole or moles than when we first started. Can I come over to your home this weekend?"

"No, Lena's family will be visiting us this weekend, how about the following Saturday? We can spend an entire day of it together going over my files."

"That will be fine. Well, I'll see you on Monday, then."

That was not to be. The results of kicking over this particular hornet's nest were about to become clearly evident.

13

THINGS GET INTERESTING

I had an uneventful weekend. I didn't even notice that someone had now placed me under very close surveillance. I happily went shopping, visited the Zoo, and walked through the Schoenbrunn Palace grounds, blissfully unaware of the profound changes that were about to come about in my life.

On Monday morning I showed up at the Ministry of Interior building as usual and headed up to Franz's office. I knocked and immediately opened the door, as had become my habit, and was very surprised to see someone else sitting in Franz's chair. It was Dr. Dorn's secretary, Nico.

He looked up from the papers he was riffling through on the desk and said, "Ah, Herr Connor, it is so good to see you again. Your presence here has just made one of the tasks I need to accomplish today much easier. Please sit down. Can I offer you a coffee?"

I was so shocked to see Nico at the desk instead of Franz, that I refused the offer. It broke my routine of starting every day at the Ministry of Interior building with a cup of coffee. I sat heavily in the visitor's chair and asked, "Where's Captain Lehner?"

"Ah, but it's not Captain Lehner anymore. I know you will be very happy to hear that it's now Major Lehner. In any case, Major Lehner is not in the Ministry building. He has been given a new post in the Federal Police and he was very anxious to assume his new position immediately. In fact, I am assisting him by clearing out his office and packing up his personal effects."

I was literally speechless and I sat gaping at Nico for quite some time. So, he just went back to going through papers on Franz's desk, effectively ignoring me for the moment.

Finally I gathered my wits about me sufficiently to ask a cogent question: "Where is Captain, er, Major Lehner's new posting?"

"Ah, yes, the Major's new posting – well, I'm sure you will be very pleased to hear that Major Lehner has been made the Chief of Police of Bregenz. He has worked very hard for the Federal Police for many years and his work has now been richly rewarded. I'm sure his family is just as excited as Major Lehner for the new opportunities that will be available to them all by living in this wonderful city. Are you familiar with Bregenz?"

"No, I'm not."

"Ah, it really is a very fine little city. It's the capital of Vorarlberg, the very westernmost province of Austria. It's located right on the shore of Lake Constance, which is one of the largest lakes in all of Europe. There is a splendid music festival held there every summer on a magnificent floating stage on the lake. There is also wonderful skiing in the winter on Pfander Mountain. The city is located right at the foot of this mountain. Yes, I'm sure that the Major and his family are feeling very fortunate, indeed, to be able to live in such a pleasant city."

Franz was now in the "very westernmost province of Austria." That meant that he was now as far away from me as possible while still remaining in Austria. It would take an all-day train trip to get there. I could forget about visiting him this weekend. My mind whirled with all the possibilities. He was now a Chief of Police. That meant he was no longer in STAPO, but instead was now part of the regular uniformed service of the Federal Police. He was going to be completely out of the loop, both physically and organizationally, for finding any moles in STAPO. Was this a coincidence, or had we both set something more sinister in motion?

I hesitated, and then said: "You mentioned a task that I had just made easier for you. Was that task telling me about Major Lehner's promotion and relocation?"

"No, as a matter of fact Dr. Dorn asked me to extend his personal thanks to you for the many months you have spent observing the activities and operations of the Federal Police. He hopes that you will be taking home some valuable lessons you may have learned by watching us in action. He also wanted me to apologize for his not being able to personally wish you a most heartfelt bon voyage."

"Bon voyage?"

"Yes, your work here has been completed and we are most grateful to you for all of the hours you have put into studying the Federal Police. If you will please hand me your visitor's pass, I would be honored to personally walk you out of the building, shake your hand, and wish you the best of luck in all your future activities."

With that Nico reached out his hand. I took off my badge and handed it to him and he immediately stood up and opened the office door for me. We then walked downstairs to the lobby and out the massive building doors. As promised, he shook my hand, this time with a truly bone crushing grip, and smiled thinly as I winced. He then laughed, turned on his heels, and walked back into the Ministry. So this was it – it all ended with a whimper and not a bang!

I walked to the subway wondering what the heck I was going to do now. I was less than half a year into what had been planned to be a three-year assignment. What had really happened to Franz? It would be way too easy to check on whether he really was a new Chief of Police, so I had to believe that much was true. It seemed to me that he had just been exiled to extreme western Austria to get him out of the way, with a promotion thrown in to keep him quiet. Would he remain quiet? It probably didn't matter if he did or not. He was no longer a part of STAPO and Nico was carefully going through his office. Was Nico a mole or just a loyal STAPO employee following orders from someone else?

When I got to the subway stop, I started to go down the steps to the platform for the train that was headed back towards my apartment. Then I suddenly realized that where I really should be going was towards the American Embassy. I needed to tell Martin about all that had just happened.

It was just past the morning rush hour and pedestrian traffic on the stairs was light, so I quickly turned around and headed back up them. As I did, I saw a man at the top of the stairs stop, hesitate, and then continue down the stairs towards me. His actions triggered a memory of mine of the far too brief introduction I had at The Farm to counter-surveillance techniques.

Had this man been following me? He had on a Tyrolean style jacket and hat. The jacket was gray with the little stand up collar typical of that style. The hat was dark green and looked like a traditional Austrian country hat. He was in his early twenties, looked tall and very fit, and now was positively bounding down the stairs like he was afraid he would miss his train. He quickly passed by me and headed onto the westbound platform.

I continued up the stairs and at the top turned and looked back down them. I didn't see the man again, but if this was a professional multi-person surveillance team, I wouldn't. One or more of the other team members would pick me up and the surveillance would just continue. Of course, all this could just be my very active imagination, but I doubted it.

The Tyrolean man looked like he had been following me, had been temporarily surprised by my sudden change in direction, and then pulled himself together and continued on like he had no interest in me. Now I wished I had received more training in counter-surveillance, or even that I just remembered more of the little I had actually been taught. One thing I did remember was that if you had discovered you were under surveillance the last thing you wanted was for the watchers to be made aware of this fact. So, I just went down the stairs to the eastbound platform and waited for the U-Bahn that would take me to the US Embassy.

During my trip to the Embassy, I tried to very discreetly check for tails, but I really couldn't spot anyone. I finally got to the Embassy and asked to see Martin. After a short wait, one of his staff escorted me into his office where Martin awaited me with a quizzical look on his face.

He said, "What's up, Stephen?"

I told him all of what had just happened, including my encounter with the Tyrolean gentlemen.

Martin gave out a long whistle and said, "Man, you've really stirred things up! Well at least Franz got a big promotion out of this mess. However, it sounds to me like you are now persona non-grata with STAPO. I'm afraid we have no choice now but to get Langley fully in the loop and see what they have to say. I'm going to need to spend the rest of the day composing a report to them about all the crap you've stepped into. You want to help me."

"Certainly, I'll do anything I can to help."

We spent the rest of the day, with only a few interruptions from Martin's staff, and wrote out a detailed report of all of my experiences with Franz, the Federal Police, and STAPO. Martin then sent it to the communications center to be encoded and sent to Langley.

"Well, Stephen, the only thing for you to do now is to go home and relax. I have a feeling it's going to take Langley at least a few days to come to a decision on what, if anything, we are to do now. I've got to change my clothes and get ready to attend a reception here at the Embassy. We're getting a new Commercial Officer who is transferring in from our Embassy in Indonesia. He was actually born in Vienna and seems to have lots of friends in high-places in the Austrian government, so we are all expecting great things from him."

Martin didn't mention his name right then, but it was Jonas Bauer. He was the KGB agent for whom Harri Aalto would eventually be acting as controller. Of course, none of us knew this at the time.

So, I did as instructed and went home. I actually ended up spending an entire week goofing off. I knew that one of the possible choices that Headquarters might make was to recall me home immediately. I tried to see all of the tourist sites in Vienna that I had been putting off seeing, assuming I would be there for years. I even attended an opera, something I had never done before, at the amazing Staatsoper opera house. I went back and visited the Schoenbrunn Palace again and walked every foot of its beautiful grounds. I visited the huge Stephansdom cathedral and the Kuntshistoriches museum of fine art. I saw the modern art collections of the MuseumsQuartier. I ate lunch at the Naschmarkt and had dinner at Beethoven Hof – a house Beethoven had lived in and which now was a Heurige. I didn't have any Sturm, there, though.

While doing all these things I kept my eye out for watchers, but couldn't spot anyone. Either I was alone or they were very professional watchers, indeed. I greatly feared that the later was true. I even found out the address of the Bregenz Police Headquarters and wrote a letter to Franz. I keep its contents very light and focused on congratulating him on his promotion, but at least he would know that I was still thinking about him.

Finally I got a call one Saturday morning from Martin inviting me out for lunch. He asked me to meet him at the Café Mozart at 1:30 PM. When I arrived, I found it to be crowded with tourists. I finally saw Martin sitting at the obligatory table in a far corner of the café and joined him. He laughed and said: "So, how do you like this place? Graham Greene loved having coffee here when he was working on the script for 'The Third Man', and even had the place featured in the film. I couldn't think of a better place for a cloak and dagger meeting."

I certainly appreciated his wacky sense of humor and so laughed along with him. Suddenly a waiter appeared and gave Martin a note. Martin's look immediately became very serious and he said: "This is from one of my staff. We actually followed you here from quite a ways back to check if you were being tailed. You were and it's a very large and professional team that's doing it. They think it is STAPO."

"Oh, great," I said.

"Nothing to worry about. I finally got word from Langley about our little situation here. To say they were unhappy at first is to put it very mildly. Apparently your tour here was supposed to be something of a paid vacation for you and they don't like it when employees don't meet their expectations. However, cooler heads in the Directorate of Operations finally prevailed over those in the Directorate of Intelligence and they've decided to run with what has been dropped in our laps."

"So, the first thing we are going to do is to set up a branch office of the Department of Defense Special Investigations Section at the Embassy. It's going to be a very small branch staffed by a single agent: you. The official reason given for its existence is to support background investigations of DOD employees and military personnel who require security clearances, and who have been born in, traveled to, or has family living in Austria. The Ambassador will be making an official request to the Austrian government in the next few days to allow said office to make information requests to the Federal Police to confirm all pertinent information provided by the applicants. This, I'm sure, is going to be granted, as there is no reason for the Austrian Foreign Office to object. It should also, in turn, cause major heartburn for the mole or moles in STAPO. You will be that bad penny that keeps turning up no matter how hard they try and get rid of it."

"We are also starting up an extremely, and I really mean extremely, discreet investigation of Dr. Dorn. I don't need to tell you what a diplomatic disaster it would be for any investigation we might conduct on the head of STAPO to be discovered by the Austrians. Right now I think he's either a KGB agent, or for some reason is turning a blind eye to one or more KGB agents in his organization. That's what we are going to try and determine, but it's likely to take an extremely long time, as we need to be very circumspect in doing so. The only reason the Directorate of Operations is taking the risk to do this is that they would love to have the opportunity to turn him into a double agent. They are positively drooling at the idea of having someone under their control who is both a high-level KGB agent and the head of STAPO. That would be an intelligence wet dream."

"So, my fine friend, how do you feel about performing the role of a staked goat? I call you a staked goat because you will be the person who we constantly stick down the craw of STAPO to hold their attention and possibly draw out the tigers hiding within there. Of course, sometimes the tiger eats the staked goat before the hunters can shoot the cat, so we are giving you the choice to back out. It goes without saying that we actually don't feel you are in any real danger, and that I would personally be heartbroken if you so much as broke a fingernail in any tussles with the KGB. We will do all that we can to assure your safety. All you will have to do is to run the occasional background query through our friends at the Federal Police and make yourself a general pest to STAPO wherever possible. The Directorate of Operations will do the rest. What do you say?"

Well, here was the chance to do what I had always said I wanted to do. I would be involved in a real espionage operation, actually playing a real role in it. Of course I wanted to do it!

"I'll gladly be your staked goat."

"I knew you would say 'yes'. So, please report to the Embassy at 9:00 AM on Monday and we will have an office ready for you, complete with DOD SIS painted on the door. Then just keep on being a major pain in the ass for STAPO and while they are watching you, we'll be sneaking in the back door and stealing all of their best silverware."

We both laughed more than it was worth at this childish joke, and I suddenly realized that what I had signed up for might be somewhat dangerous and that I was actually a little scared. Somehow that made it even more desirable to me. I'd gone too many years living a completely safe existence. It was time to be a little scared as I could already see that it would make my life more enjoyable to occasionally be frightened.

"Just remember, we are going to have to go super, super slowly on this whole investigation and it may very well take years for us to get any definitive answers. In the meantime, I suggest you contact your friend Major Lehner and set up a visit with him at this new home sometime in the coming weeks. We would love to see that file he showed you, and if you can convince him to give it to you, that would be truly magnificent."

"I already wrote him last week, congratulating him on his promotion."

"Great, well when he replies, be sure to ask him if you can visit him when he and his family are finally settled in their new home."

Monday morning saw me at the Embassy at 8:30 AM. I was early again, as I usually am, but I was nevertheless able to find out where my new office was located within the Embassy. Of course, it was in the basement. It did have a door with "DOD SIS" painted on it, as promised. When I opened the door I saw a tiny office with a desk with a swivel chair, a secure filing cabinet with combination lock, and a trash can. It was about all there was room for in this little space. The desk had a blotter, an inbox, and a phone. This office clearly violated Austrian law because it had no window. However, as the US Embassy was treated as the sovereign soil of the United States, I could legally be consigned to work in this dungeon. I sat down in my chair and discovered that at least it was a comfortable one. I checked my desk's drawers and found that they were all empty. I didn't even have a pen other than the personal one I usually carried in my shirt pocket. My office didn't even belong on the same planet as Dr. Dorn's, but it was all mine and I was grateful to have it. It meant that I was going to be able to continue to live and work in Vienna and that I was going to be part of a complex and important intelligence operation. Looking at it in that light it seemed to be a very fine office, indeed.

A little after 9:00 AM Martin dropped by for a visit. He had to try very hard not to laugh at the tiny basement office I had been assigned. "Hey, I'm amazed they found a private office of any kind for you. We're pretty jammed up for room here in the Embassy," he said sympathetically to me.

"No problem, it's really all that's necessary for my cover story. I don't imagine that I'm going to have to be doing all that much real work here. However, if anyone actually checks they will discover that, yes, I do have an actual office at the Embassy. So, what's the first order of business for today."

"Well for now, you'll just have to come here everyday for show. I don't believe we've received the official OK from the Austrian Foreign Office for you to work with the Federal Police on background checks. I doubt whether it will take much longer, though."

He grinned and said: "I imagine there has been some push back from STAPO regarding the Federal Police supporting the DOD SIS, but I don't see how this can prevent the request from eventually being approved. There is just no logical reason why it shouldn't be. So, in the meantime, bring lots of reading material with you from home and show up every day. Who knows, you might even get a phone call from one of your great friends at STAPO inquiring as to your well-being. You wouldn't want to miss that!"

So, that's what I did. I showed up at the Embassy every weekday by no later than 9:00 AM and left no earlier than 5:00 PM. I brought books and magazines to keep me busy. Soon, an envelope containing some security applications appeared in my inbox. They would all be for real people with an authentic past connection to Austria. They had to be in order to pass scrutiny by the Federal Police. However, when I reviewed them I discovered that they all seemed to actually be for new State Department personnel recently assigned to the Embassy. One application was even for the new Commercial Officer at the Embassy that Martin had told me about: Jonas Bauer. He had been born in Vienna and so definitely had a connection to this country.

It didn't seem reasonable to me that the DOD would be clearing Embassy personnel. Perhaps whoever at the Directorate of Operations put this stuff together was desperate for relevant and realistic material and just did the best he could on such short notice. So, I just waited for the OK to take my haul to the Federal Police and request their assistance. I was really looking forward to doing so, regardless of what it contained.

It actually ended up taking four weeks before we got the approval from the Austrian Foreign Office to submit our requests. Someone at STAPO must have fought tooth and nail to prevent it, but must have been finally overruled. I was instructed to bring all of my background check requests to, of all people, Dr. Dorn's secretary, Nico. It looked like someone at STAPO wanted to keep a very close eye on my interactions with the Federal Police. It would really be good to see jolly Nico again.

I called the number that had been given to us and I heard Nico's voice on the line. "Nico, this is Stephen Connor calling from the US Embassy. How are you?"

There was complete silence on the line. I waited a short while and then said, "Hello?"

Finally Nico said, "Ah, Herr Connor, I am very busy today. Why are you calling?"

"I'm calling you to ask for an appointment to bring over some requests for background checks. I understood that this had all been approved by your Foreign Office. Are you aware of this?"

There was another long pause, and then Nico said: "Yes, I am. You may come here in one hour." With that, he hung up.

Well, this wasn't anywhere near the joyous and friendly reception I had hoped for, but at least I had an appointment with Nico. This was going to be fun.

A little less than one hour later, I was in the lobby of the Ministry of Interior building and asked to see Nico. The guard at the front desk seemed surprised to see me again. He called Nico and got approval to send me upstairs to his office. So, I got my visitor's badge and virtually bounded up the stairs with happiness and not a little excitement. Soon I was at Nico's open doorway.

"Nico, it's so good to see you again!"

Nico looked up at me with an extremely unhappy look on his face. No, it was more than an unhappy look. It reminded me of the look that the CIA analyst Larry had given me – one of pure hatred. Nico didn't like me one bit. "Please give me your requests," was all that he said.

I opened my briefcase and handed the forms to him. I then said, "All we want is for the Federal Police to confirm the information that was provided to us, plus provide any information regarding any criminal records or other information that might cast doubt regarding a person's good character."

Nico jerked the forms our of my hand and said, "Yes, yes, I know what you want. I will call you when the results come back. It shouldn't take more than a day or two. What is your phone number?"

I gave him my office phone number. I also said, "You will be able to reach me at my Embassy office any weekday between 9:00 AM and 5:00 PM. You are more than welcome to visit me there. I'd love to show you my office. Have you been to the Embassy before?"

Nico virtually growled, "No, I'm afraid I have many pressing tasks to complete today, so I must bid you adieu." With that he placed my requests into a desk drawer, picked up some other papers on his desk, and began reading them very intently.

"Goodbye, Nico, I hope you have a wonderful day," I said and left the grumpy Nico. With that I made my way back to the Embassy actually whistling a happy tune. This was turning out to all be great fun. Then I remembered that I hadn't heard anything from Franz, and my happy feeling quickly evaporated. What had happened to him? Should I try and call him? Maybe I needed to speak with Martin on how to proceed.

14

THE KGB PITCHES A FIT AND I TAKE A TRAIN RIDE

The KGB soon had copies of all of the background check requests I had submitted to Nico. They absolutely had a fit to see that one of them was for their prized agent: Jonas Bauer. What was I trying to pull here? Was I trying to rub their noses in the fact that I knew that he was actually a KGB agent? If I knew, why would I reveal that knowledge to the KGB? What possible motive could I have? Why hadn't Jonas simply been sent back to the US and arrested? What inexplicably devious plan was unfolding before their eyes? Had I managed to turn him into a double agent? If so, why would I be letting on that I knew him to be a KGB agent? None of this made any sense to them.

Cables shot back and forth between the KGB Residence in the Soviet Embassy and Moscow. Everyone was completely baffled by what I might be trying to accomplish. One thing was immediately clear, though – the KGB had to warn Jonas that he might have been compromised. He must cease all further contact with the KGB for the time being.

Plans were also put into place for a possible emergency exfiltration of Bauer's illegal control: Harri Aalto. A fast car could get him to the Czech border in less than an hour, so one was put in place near his hotel in case it was ever needed.

Everyone connected with the KGB operations in Vienna was virtually hysterical over what was now happening there. A special committee was formed in the Second Chief Directorate headquarters to consider their options for dealing with this crisis.

All of the material they had gathered on me was presented to this committee. It was pretty scant. One interesting piece of information they had turned up was the Iranian fatwa that called for my death. This piece of information might prove very valuable in coming up with a plan for dealing with me. They couldn't simply kill me. However, if an Iranian, or someone who appeared to be Iranian, were to kill me, then no blame could be put on the KGB and the problem of Stephen Connor would go away forever.

Of course, this would be an extremely dangerous breach of the unofficial truce between the CIA and KGB, and since I seemed to be a very important agent to the CIA with the ear of the President, they decided to not to kill me. However, they soon came up with another idea – an idea that was much more subtle but might neutralize me just as effectively. Work on putting this plan into operation was to be started as soon as all the necessary resources could be brought onto the scene.

In addition, the committee decided not to offer asylum to Jonas Bauer. He appeared to be working strictly for money and not political motives and thus it was quite likely that he would refuse asylum. In addition, although he had done some helpful work in the past for the KGB, his Vienna assignment was the first in which he might be able to provide really important information to them. He had only been a KGB agent for less than 3 years and had actually produced little really valuable intelligence so far. His friendship with Austrians in high-level government positions and his new job at the US Embassy should result in huge quantities of top grade information. He was still at the Embassy in his Commercial Officer position and he still had his freedom, so for the moment the KGB was not ready to throw away all that they had invested in him. There appeared to be nothing more that could be done other than to wait and see what developed and suspend all contact with him for the time being.

Meanwhile, I had conferred with Martin about the fact that Franz had never responded to my letter. Martin suggested that I give him a telephone call and make one more attempt to reconnect with him. If that didn't go well, I should just drop any further attempts to re-establish our relationship. There was no reason to press him and possibly put him or his family in any possible danger. Martin managed to get Franz's new home phone number and so that evening I tried calling him from my apartment. He answered on the second ring.

"Franz, this is Stephen, congratulations on your promotion. How are you?"

"Stephen, it's so good to hear from you! How are you? Where are you?"

"I'm still in Vienna in the same apartment. My work in studying the operations of the Federal Police has ended, but I now have a job at the American Embassy here. I love Vienna and wasn't ready to leave it, so I managed to wangle a way to stay. How is your new job and your new home?"

"Oh, the job is very challenging. You would think being the Chief of Police of a little city like Bregenz would be a lark, but it's really a lot of work. We are in the process of going through a major reorganization here and everything is quite chaotic. On top of that, I've had to arrange the sale of our house in Vienna. Right now we are renting a house in Bregenz until we can decide exactly where we want to live. The city itself is marvelous, right at the foot of some beautiful mountains and right on Lake Constance. It's a huge lake that sits between Austria, West Germany, and Switzerland. It's also a wonderful route for smugglers, but enough of my problems. How are you doing? A new job with the Embassy?"

"At the Embassy, really. I'm still with the DOD SIS. They just decided to open an office in Vienna to support background checks and they are letting me work there. I still get to regularly visit your Federal Police headquarters in the Ministry building."

Franz was silent for a few moments and then said, "Well, if you're not too busy, perhaps you could come visit us some day. I know Lena would love to see you again and we have a spare bedroom that we can put you in. How about it? Any possibility of that happening? Bregenz is truly beautiful and I know you would love it here as much as we do."

"I would love to come visit you, if you're willing to put up with me staying in your home. I actually was planning on taking a few days vacation in the next week or two. Would that be a convenient time for you?"

"Absolutely, the sooner the better. You must see me in my new Chief of Police uniform, you will be truly awed by it," Franz said and laughed.

So, we arranged for me to spend a day at his home. He could afford to take a day off from his new job, but no more than one day. Franz suggested that I take the train. It would take over eight hours and two changes of trains to get there, but the trip would take me through the length of Austria and I would see some truly beautiful sights along the way. I would take a day getting there, spend the entire next day with Franz and his family, and return to Vienna on the third day.

I immediately let Martin know that the trip was on for next week. He said, "OK, your sole mission is to get his file, if that's in anyway possible. Just be very careful of what you say and do while you are there. Assume you'll be watched and listened to the entire time. Be as careful and discreet as you possibly can be and be sure that you don't do anything that would endanger Chief Lehner or his family."

"I would never do that, I'd lay down my own life first," I said, and then realized that I would. I wasn't just saying it to sound brave, I really felt that way. That surprised me. This job was changing me in ways I found quite extraordinary.

Two days later, a Federal Police officer showed up at the Embassy asking for me. I met him in the lobby and he handed me a folio and a receipt for me to sign. I opened the folio to see all of the security clearance applications I had left with Nico, along with a report from the Federal Police on each one of the applicants. I signed the receipt and thanked the officer. I took the whole lot to Martin and we went over it together.

After reviewing all the material, Martin said, "Well, it doesn't look like there is anything significant here. It appears as though the Federal Police actually did check the backgrounds of all of these people and just gave us everything they had on file for them – which is practically nothing. Oh wait; you submitted a background check request for our new Commercial Officer? That's a riot! What do the Police have to say about him – any skeletons in his closet?"

He scrutinized the report on Jonas Bauer with obvious amusement. "This must have confused the heck out of the Federal Police – the DOD doing background checks on currently employed State Department staff. Was that your brilliant idea?"

"No, somebody in the Directorate of Operations put this package together and sent it all to me. I think whoever it was lacks imagination."

We both had a good laugh over this, never thinking for a moment that these somewhat ridiculous requests were causing an uproar in the KGB. In any case, Jonas' report came back clean and so Martin dropped the whole subject and we again went over plans for my trip to visit Franz.

The next Monday I made my way to the Westbahnhof, the western railroad station in Vienna. It was an immense structure and it wasn't even the largest railroad station in the city. It had eleven tracks completely enclosed inside it and over forty thousand travelers used it every day.

In order to get to Bregenz, I would need to take three trains: a train to Salzburg, then Innsbruck, and finally Bregenz. This was my first experience with railroads in Austria and I was about to be very impressed. First of all, I had my choice of twenty trains leaving the Westbahnhof each day that could get me to Bregenz. There was that much available train service. Second, I noticed that my itinerary showed my connection in Salzburg to be only five minutes – that is my train from Vienna was scheduled to arrive just five minutes before the train to Innsbruck was scheduled to leave. Winter was just starting with light snows already hitting Vienna and this seemed like an impossibly tight connection. Third, the trains themselves were absolutely luxurious with large warm compartments with lots of space for luggage and extremely comfortable seats.

Of course, my train left Vienna exactly on time. It arrived in Salzburg exactly on time, with the train to Innsbruck sitting right across the platform for ease in moving from one train to the other. No surprise any longer - the Innsbruck train left exactly on time, and the train from Innsbruck to Bregenz also left and arrived exactly on time. Why can't trains in the US come anywhere near this level of performance? The Austrians seemed to have achieved railroad perfection.

I spent over eight hours on the trains, yet enjoyed every minute of it. I arrived in Bregenz relaxed and invigorated by my journey. The trains were clean, quiet, comfortable, and the food served on them was really excellent. By now it was November 1979 with winter starting to get it's grip on Austria, so I was also treated to incredible scenic winter views along the way featuring snow covered farms, towns, snow capped mountains, frozen lakes, streams, and some very long tunnels. I had a blast. I thought that this must be the very best way to travel anywhere.

Franz was waiting for me at the train station. Only a little snow covered the city, I had expected more. I was also disappointed not to see him in his new uniform, as he was wearing casual civilian clothing.

"Stephen, how good to see you again," he shouted as he embraced me. The other Austrians on the platform looked somewhat askance at this behavior, but that was just the way Franz was. He insisted on personally carrying my only piece of luggage to his car and we were soon on our way to his new home.

I motioned about in the car in a pantomime of asking if he thought it was bugged. He put his finger to his lips and so I took that as a definite maybe, and we kept the conversation light on the way to the house. We were at his new home in less than fifteen minutes and it was truly a beautiful house.

It was much larger than his house in Vienna. It was a large single story home with a real country look and feel about it. The view from it was even more impressive. Before us was the giant Lake Constance. Behind us was Pfander Mountain, whose snow-covered peaks were almost four thousand feet in elevation. To the right was West Germany, and to the left Switzerland. The Alpine peaks around us were all covered with brilliant snow packs. At night the entire city was lit up in an astonishing variety of colored lights. This was one of the prettiest spots I have ever seen.

Lena greeted us at the door and gave me a hug. Christine and Albert made their mandatory brief appearance and then vanished. Lena showed me my room and Franz brought my suitcase into it. I was shown the bathroom and invited to change and freshen up for dinner. I did so gratefully.

Dinner was as I had come to expect of any food prepared by Lena: amazingly delicious. Lena had cooked us a meal of roast trout with parsley potatoes, and an amazing pancake dessert with stewed plums. I marveled at how Franz managed to maintain the physique of a long-distance runner when his wife served him such food. I would have weighed three hundred pounds if I were married to her.

We sat up late that night talking in front of a raging fire in the fireplace and drinking beer. Franz and Lena excitedly told me all about Bregenz and the surrounding region and how much happier they were living there instead of in Vienna. They said the opportunities for outdoor recreation were virtually limitless and they felt it was a much better environment for the children. Franz even spoke of buying a small boat for cruising Lake Constance in the summer. They both seemed genuinely glad to be in their new home. Franz complained slightly about the bureaucratic and political demands of his new job, but he was also bursting with pride over having attained this lofty position in the Federal Police. It was quite late before we finally turned in for the night.

The next morning we got up a little later than originally planned, but we were soon all in the kitchen enjoying croissants, sweet pastries, coffee, and juice. The children even ate with us and soon joined in on the laughing and joking. We planned to take the cable car up to the top of Pfander Mountain that day and play in the snow. Lena and the children would ski, but since I didn't ski Franz and I would race down the mountain on sleds instead. After breakfast Franz and I went to his new study – a much larger one than he had in Vienna. He invited me to sit on the familiar couch I had occupied in Vienna and put another Bugs Bunny cartoon into the VCR. He closed the door and turned up the volume on the TV.

He then quickly sat down next to me and said, "What the hell is going on, Stephen? I was told that you had left Austria. I was completely shocked when you called me."

"You didn't get my letter?"

"No, what letter?"

"I sent you a letter congratulating you on your promotion and new job shortly after you left Vienna."

"I never received it. Is my mail being intercepted?"

"Perhaps. Anyway, Franz, how did you end up here?"

"The weekend we couldn't meet, when Lena's relatives were visiting, on

Saturday morning I got a call from the Director of the Federal Police and was asked to meet with him that very day. He told me that he had been having serious problems with law enforcement in Bregenz, had sacked the Chief of Police there, and had just started searching for a replacement. He told me that Dr. Dorn had recommended that I be given the position and agreed to release me from my duties in STAPO right away. Apparently Dr. Dorn also convinced him that things had become so bad in Bregenz that I should be immediately sent here, with my family to follow when they could. So, he gave me the job on the spot under the condition that I would fly to Bregenz the very next morning on a Federal Police aircraft and start work immediately there the first thing Monday morning. He said that conditions there had deteriorated gravely and that I'd have a tough job."

"It was a huge promotion for me and I really couldn't imagine turning it down. Frankly, I was also relieved to be getting out of STAPO, especially after we seemed to be making no progress in finding our mole. I readily accepted. The strange thing was when I arrived I didn't really find all that many problems at the station. They were a little disorganized, but things had really been running pretty well under the Assistant Chief. It was only then that I started to think that I had actually been sent here to get me out of STAPO. However, from a very selfish point of view it's been a very positive change for my family and me. Bregenz really is a wonderful place for us to live and it's practically unheard of in the Federal Police for anyone to receive a promotion such as I did. Are you angry at me for accepting it?"

"Absolutely not, I think it's great that everything has turned out so well for you and your family. I'm really very happy for all of you."

"Thank you, Stephen, that's a huge relief to me. I dragged you here to Austria to help me find a mole, and then I left you on your own. I've been feeling that I let you down. Now tell me what you've been doing? How did you manage to stay in Austria?"

I filled him in on what had happened to me since he had been gone. I then asked him if he still had his file.

"Yes, I do. It's in my safe at the station. I was planning on briefly visiting the station later today just to check that everything is OK in spite of my absence, and I'll get it for you then."

After this conversation we left the house and ended up having a great day together. The view from the top of Pfander Mountain was truly magnificent. The entire town was laid out below us. Lake Constance was so enormous that we couldn't see the end of it even from this lofty perch, and the lake was completely free of ice. Seemingly endless snow capped Alps were visible to the south. The air was crisp and cold but we were all bundled up in snow gear and woolen caps.

Lena and the children skied like Olympic champions. Skiing was the national sport in Austria and everyone there seemed to ski like a professional. Franz and I had crazy races down the mountain on sleds we rented and by the time the day was nearing its end all of us were close to exhaustion from our playful exertions.

After riding the cable car back down, we all got into Franz's car and headed home. He dropped us all off at the house while he continued onto the station. Lena made hot chocolate and snacks for the children and me and I helped get a fire going in the fireplace.

Franz returned in about an hour. As soon as I saw him enter the house, I knew something was wrong.

"It's gone," he gasped.

"Why am I not surprised?"

Franz briefly chatted with Lena and then took me into his study. The routine of the loud Bugs Bunny cartoon was repeated and then Franz sat next to me and blurted out, "I can't believe it! It's gone! All my work gone! I've been an idiot; I should have never left it in my safe. What a fool I am!"

He was so shaken that I immediately tried to console him: "It's OK, Franz. It's not that important. We're sure about your conclusions and an investigation is already progressing at a very cautious and careful pace. The file would have been nice to have, but it's not that important."

I wasn't really sure if what I had said was true or not, but Franz was so upset that I felt that I had to say it anyway.

"Who had access to your safe?"

"No one is supposed to have the combination but me and the Assistant Chief. The combination was changed when I started working here – wait, so the locksmith we called also could have it. Anyway, I really don't know, Stephen, things are still somewhat disorganized and chaotic at the station. Maybe the Assistant Chief was careless about where he kept it. For all I know it's written on his desk blotter. I was a complete fool to trust that it would be safe there."

"Again, it's not that important. The really important thing is that whoever took it now knows exactly what you know about the KGB penetration of STAPO. You've got to be on your guard now. I think it's not too outrageous for me to suggest that you should arrange for a security detail for Lena and the kids. It's probably not really necessary because you are now out of STAPO and they have you out here in the boonies, but if I were you that's exactly what I would do. What do you think?"

"Oh my God, have I put my family in danger?"

"I really don't know, and probably not, but I think it's a good idea to take whatever measures you can to ensure their safety."

Franz finally pulled himself together and said, "Yes, I think you are right. I think I've already found out whom I can count on here and I'll arrange to put together a discreet security detail using some of my best young officers working in plainclothes. My God, what have I done?"

"It's OK, Franz, I'm probably being way too cautious, but I don't think it would hurt to do so. Come up with some excuse to need security for your family, at least for a while."

"Thanks, Stephen, I'll do that."

The rest of my time with Franz was spent with a black cloud of guilt and concern hanging over him. We had a very quiet dinner that night. Franz would arrange for security when returning to work the next day, but in the meantime he was carrying his pistol at all times, whether inside or outside of the house. I always did anyway, so that meant that his family had two armed men protecting them while I was there.

The next day it was Lena who took me to the railroad station. We drove in Franz's car with the kids sitting very quietly in the back seat. Franz had left very early that morning for the station and been picked up by one of his patrol cars. By the time we were ready to leave for the railroad station, two of his officers had arrived at the house and then followed us to the station in an unmarked car. Lena looked a little shaken, but she was putting on a brave face and pretending that having armed bodyguards was the most normal thing in the world. The kids seemed oblivious to the whole situation.

Lena hugged me goodbye at the station and I boarded my train. The trip back to Vienna seemed far less enjoyable than the original trip out had been. What a mess everything had become. I truly hoped that neither Franz nor his family would be hurt because of what he had discovered and documented with such care.

After I arrived back in Vienna I was back at the Embassy again and immediately briefed Martin. He tried to brush off the whole situation, but I think inside he was just as concerned as I was. At least Franz had an entire city police force at his disposal for protecting his family.

15

THE INVESTIGATION DRAGS ON AND ON

So, the next few months dragged on at what truly seemed like a snail's pace. I kept in touch with Franz and he reported that all was well. He had made up some story about being threatened by a smuggling gang and so was able to keep protection in place for his family. Nothing untoward had happened to them, or to him. Everything seemed the height of normality. I finally started thinking that maybe losing his file about the penetration of STAPO by the KGB might actually have ended up making him safer. Since he was now completely out of the picture there really was no reason for them to harm him. Nevertheless, I was happy he was still taking every possible precaution to ensure his safety and the safety of his family.

I kept meeting with Martin and asking what was happening with the investigation of Dr. Dorn, but all he ever could say was that things were still proceeding slowly and cautiously and that we all had to be patient. I regularly received security clearance applications for background checks every few weeks, and dutifully passed them on to Nico. I noticed that all of the ones I was now receiving actually appeared to be for DOD employees and military personnel, instead of the ridiculous State Department applications that we had first used. Nico dutifully responded to all of the requests and returned them with the Federal Police findings within a couple of days of receiving them. So, it went - day after day, week after week, and month after month.

I was getting sick of coming to work, closing my door, and reading books and magazines. I was seriously thinking of smuggling a small TV into my office to help me fill my daily "work" hours with something more entertaining. I really missed having an intelligence analyst workstation available to me. At least that would have been able to constantly provide me with interesting new information about the KGB. As it was, I was pretty much in the dark about everything that was going on.

My only duty was to keep in the face of the STAPO and hope that would somehow provoke the KGB. I really had no idea of what progress, if any, was being made in finding the mole or moles within STAPO. I was getting bored out of my mind. I had to think of something to do to occupy myself or I thought I would go crazy. I started trying to think up something that I could do to speed up the investigation or force the KGB into to doing something, anything, which might reveal useful information to us. I needn't have bothered though, because the KGB was finally about to make its move against me.

One Saturday morning I was sitting in a local coffee house near my apartment enjoying some sweet pastries and coffee, and reading the International Herald Tribune. It was about the only English language newspaper I could easily find in Vienna and I really relished reading it. It had been providing news to American expatriates since the 1920s. Hemingway even mentioned it in his 1926 novel "The Sun Also Rises". I felt very Hemingway-esque whenever I read it. It had become a ritual for me to have coffee and pastries along with the International Herald Tribune every Saturday morning.

The coffee house was crowded, as usual for this time of day. So, I wasn't all that surprised when an attractive young woman asked if she might join me at my table. She did so in English. I assumed she must have noticed my American newspaper.

She said with only a slight German accent: "Excuse me, may I join you?"

"Please do," I replied, and rearranged the contents of the table to make room for her. She took off her winter coat and hung it up on a hook on the wall. She stuffed her woolen cap into one of its pockets.

She looked to be in her early twenties. She was extremely petite; probably not much over five foot two inches in height. She was dressed like a student with a black and white skirt, black tights, black winter boots, a colorful blouse, a tan leather vest, and she had short blonde hair. She had an extremely delicate figure and appeared quite feminine and very attractive. She was carrying a copy of one of the local newspapers, the Wiener Zeitung, and what appeared to be a large sketchbook. She placed them both on the table and hailed a waiter. She ordered just a coffee.

She then looked at me, smiled a radiant smile, and asked: "Are you an American?"

"Yes, I am."

"Oh, I'm simply mad about everything American," she said excitedly, and then gave a slight laugh.

"Oh, would that include me, too?"

She laughed more heartily now and said: "I'm sure it will."

With that, it all started. She told me she was a German from Berlin and was studying architecture at the University of Vienna. She wished more than anything to move to the United States someday, probably to New York City. She was filled with questions regarding everything I could tell her about what life was really like in the US.

Like most Europeans she seemed to have absolutely no idea of just how large the US really was. She talked about a two-week trip she planned to take there next year that would need to cover impossible distances in that time frame. I tried to make her realize just how ridiculous her planned itinerary was, and she eventually laughed at what she then realized was her own naivety about the true size of the United States.

The more we spoke the more I found her to be charming, energetic, intelligent, very attractive - and very young. I was thirty-two, then. She told me that she was twenty-two. Her youthful energy and exuberance made me feel positively ancient.

She then told me: "I want to go to the Schoenbrunn Palace today and make some sketches of it. Have you been there?"

"Many times," I said.

"Wonderful," she positively gushed. "Would you be my guide? I've never been there before."

Well, this was getting interesting. Was she really just looking for a little help? I was pretty old for there to be any romantic interest on her part. Did she have some ulterior motive? Did she think I would be able to somehow help get her to the US? Damn, I was getting so suspicious in my old age! Maybe she's just enjoying being with an American.

"Sure, I would be happy to do so. What is your name?"

"Ursula. What is yours?"

"Stephen."

So, we did just that. We bundled up against the February Vienna weather and took a streetcar to the Schoenbrunn Palace. There we walked about inside the palace with Ursula making frequent stops to "ooh and ah" at various architectural points of the building and make quick sketches of them. She even insisted on making a sketch of me, which was quite a good likeness even though it only took her a few minutes to dash it off in pencil on one of her sketchbook pages.

After viewing the interior of the palace, we braved the cold wind, walked up Gloriette Hill, and ate lunch at the Cafe Gloriette. It offered a beautiful view of the Palace and grounds as well as a very tasty luncheon. After lunch, Ursula said: "Stephen, where do you live?"

"Not far from here," I replied.

"Tell me all about it. What's it like, architecturally?"

So, I described the apartment I was living in and the building in which it was located. Ursula asked if we could go see it, so off we went. Upon arriving at my building, we walked around the outside of it and Ursula commented on various architectural aspects of it. Then we walked up the stairs to my apartment. She was awed by the view from there and ventured outside onto the patio deck, even though it was getting quite cold and windy by now. She seemed a little chilled when she stepped back inside, so I made us both some hot chocolate. We sat in my living room enjoying the warmth of the room and the inner warmth provided by the hot beverage.

"Stephen, you are such a nice man and have been so kind to me today, I would love to repay your kindness with a small favor. Would you allow me to cook you a dinner tonight?"

"That's really not necessary," I said. "I really enjoyed spending the day with you and that has been reward enough."

"No, please allow me to do this for you," she positively insisted.

"All right, if it will make you happy I will concede to your wishes," I said laughing and raised my hands in mock surrender.

"Wonderful, you stay here and I will walk down to the Hietzinger Haupstrasse and do some quick shopping for the ingredients I'll need."

"Hey, it's really getting cold outside, why don't you just use what I already have in the kitchen. I don't want you to freeze out there."

"Nonsense, we German girls are used to dealing with harsh climates. This is nothing compared to some of the winters I've lived through. Please, stay here and let me do this small favor for you. It will please me greatly."

So, I finally gave in a second time and let her out the door. After she left, I again wondered to myself exactly what was going on. She seemed a pleasant enough young lady and I had enjoyed her company that day. Yet I still harbored a little suspicion as to her motives and any hidden agenda she might have. Why was she being so nice to me? After fretting a short while over all of this, I finally just decided that I had been associating with double-dealing intelligence personnel for too long and decided to just take Ursula at face value.

She was a very young architecture student who obviously loved her area of study and we had just had an enjoyable day together. She wanted to do something nice for me in return for my companionship that day. I should just appreciate her kind heart and finish off a very nice day by simply enjoying the dinner she would prepare for us. After dinner I would walk her to the streetcar stop, kiss her on the check, and thank her for sharing a very wonderful day with me. Then I'd walk back home kicking myself the entire way for being such a suspicious old goat.

She returned in a little less than an hour, and I gave her a cup of hot coffee to ward off any chill. She then chased me out of my kitchen, told me to sit in the living room, turn on some music, and just relax while she prepared our dinner. She positively forbade me from helping her in any way. I was to sit and relax until summoned into the dining room to eat dinner. I obeyed her orders.

When summoned in a little over an hour, I was blown away by what she had prepared for us. There were candles lit on my dining room table and a vast feast was spread over it.

"There's no way we will be able to eat all of this food," I exclaimed.

"Hush, so you will have leftover food. When you eat it tomorrow you can think of the foolish girl you spent so much time helping today and remember her gratitude to you."

So, I sat down and she started serving me a truly memorable meal. We started off with a light cucumber salad with a sweet vinegar dressing and some red wine. She followed this up with an entree that consisted of meatballs made from pork and beef, boiled potatoes with butter, green beans with sour cream, bacon, and onions, and more red wine. Dessert was cheese with sweetened fresh fruit and an aperitif. This girl could cook and there would be lots of everything left over for tomorrow, too.

I just about wore myself out complimenting Ursula and was feeling in quite a wonderful mood due to the great food I had just eaten and all the wine we had with it. I was stuffed almost to bursting and feeling warm and contented as we retired to the living room to finish our aperitifs. I sat on the couch, and Ursula sat next to me. We looked at each other and suddenly she burst out laughing. I couldn't help but join her, although I hadn't a clue as to why she was suddenly laughing so hard. Then she leaned over and kissed me – gently at first, and then with real passion. What can I say – I returned the favor and was soon literally carrying her off to my bedroom. We made love, drifted off to sleep, woke and made love again, and I finally passed out for the rest of the night.

I awoke the next morning with a bit of a headache and wondering if I hadn't just had a very realistic dream. I looked over at the other side of my bed and it was empty. I then heard some clattering in the kitchen and decided that I had not dreamed about yesterday, but had really experienced all of it. Then Ursula came into the bedroom wearing one of my shirts. She was so petite that it looked like a dress on her, and just like something I'd only seen before in movies. She was carrying a steaming cup of coffee. As she got near me, I reached out to draw her back into bed, but she pushed me away.

"Enough of that you animal, you need breakfast to rebuild your strength. Here, drink this coffee and then get cleaned up and come into the kitchen when you are ready. I'll make you a real American breakfast. How do you like your eggs?"

"Scrambled, and please make them durch", I said somewhat groggily. I had learned the hard way that Europeans like their scrambled eggs to be very runny. If I wanted them cooked as they typically were in the US, I had to ask for them "durch", which in German literally meant "through". This got them cooked the way I liked them.

"Durch they will be then," she said with a huge smile and giggle.

I sat up, drank my coffee, and marveled at the fact that I had somehow either:

a) Miraculously acquired a beautiful young sexy girlfriend, or
b) Had just been set up to be the chump in some unknown nefarious scheme that was being hatched against me.

I doubted the former as I had never before had beautiful young women throw themselves at me. As to the scheme being hatched against me - I was completely clueless as to what it might be at that moment. However, there was no reason not to fully enjoy all the effort that was being put into lulling me into a completely languid state through great food and sex. I might as well ride this one out as far as I could safely do so. So, I got up and showered and threw on some clothes, anxiously anticipating the great breakfast I was about to be served, and also looking forward to seeing what unfolded afterward.

Of course I checked that my Sig P230 was handy, loaded, and still in functioning order. I had just discovered another great reason to pocket carry a pistol – when you rapidly and carelessly disrobed, there was no noticeable holster coming into view during that process. The pistol just stayed in your pocket when your pants came off and hit the floor.

I walked into my kitchen just at the moment when my scrambled eggs were being poured into the frying pan. Bacon and even buttered toast had already been prepared and were being kept warm in the oven. Ursula stood on tiptoes to offer me a brief kiss and then commanded me to sit down at the kitchen table. She handed me an orange juice and told me to drink it down as more coffee would soon follow.

I've got to say that whatever this girl was up to, she was a kitchen wizard and an amazing cook. Perfectly scrambled eggs, bacon, and toast were served up to me that morning. She had prepared only toast for herself, which she ate while I consumed my much more substantial meal. When I asked about her food, she just said that she wasn't that hungry and needed to shower, dress, and leave right after breakfast. She had studying to do for an exam the next day. Well, maybe all my theories were just a bunch of hooey. Maybe I had just had a simple one-night stand with a girl who was now moving on. I couldn't decide if I was relieved or disappointed.

After showering and dressing, Ursula came out and handed me a piece of paper. On it was her full name, Ursula Hauer, an address near Vienna University, and her phone number.

She kissed me more passionately this time and said, "Please come over to my apartment on Friday at 8:00 PM and bring some clothes and toiletries. I will have the entire weekend free and I have some wonderful ideas for ways we can fill it with some very pleasurable things to do. You will come, won't you? Promise?"

"Of course I will," I said with my faith in her evil intentions now fully restored. She gave me one more lingering kiss and was out the door. So, that was it – I would go to her apartment on Friday night where I would be killed, dismembered, and my body parts sold to the highest bidder. Or maybe something even worse than that. I really had no idea what this young siren might have in store for me that Friday night, but I was pretty sure that it would be something quite evil.

16

BOY, YOU'RE NOT GOING TO BELIEVE WHAT HAPPENED TO ME

I couldn't wait to call Martin and tell him what had just happened to me. So, as soon as she left I called his home. I actually woke him up, but I didn't care if he was trying to sleep-in late. I asked him if he would be free for lunch. He conferred briefly with his wife and then came back on the phone: "Is this important?"

"You are not going to believe what just happened to me, and I think you are really going to want to hear all about it as soon as you can," I replied.

There were then more mumbling sounds coming over the line and he finally came back and said: "How about meeting for a beer at around 3:00 PM? We can meet at Medl-Brau."

"Fine with me, see you at 3:00," and I hung up the phone. It was going to be a long time for me to wait as I was simply bursting to tell someone, anyone, about my amazing encounter with the young Ursula Hauer. This is why I had come to Vienna: in order to have extraordinary experiences such as I had never had before.

The day slowly crept by and I was at the beer garden by 2:30, so anxious was I to relate my adventures to Martin. He finally arrived right at 3:00 and I waved for him to come to my table. He flagged down a waiter on the way and ordered a beer.

"So, what's so damned important that you've had to completely screw up my

Sunday family plans."

I told him everything.

When I was done explaining it all, Martin exclaimed: "Holy mackerel! Did this really happen or was it all some kind of sexual fantasy you just dreamed up?"

"I've got the leftovers in my refrigerator to prove it!"

"My god, this is the most god-awful honeypot that I've ever heard the KGB put together. They are famous for this kind of crap, but someone must be really desperate to try and get you tangled up in such an obvious scheme."

A honeypot is simply the use of sex for the intelligence purposes of blackmail and/or coercion. The KGB, and its affiliated East German secret police organization, the STASI, was famous for making use of this technique. The KGB seemed to believe that all Americans were sex-obsessed materialists who could easily be entrapped by sexual lures. They even had a code name for females who had been specifically trained to act as honeypots: swallows. The STASI, in particular, usually had a substantial number of swallows ready for deployment when needed. I was starting to wonder if my new girlfriend Ursula wasn't really a STASI agent. Oh well, so much for any great budding romance with her!

I replied, "So, what do I do about my date on Friday night? What are they planning on doing to me at her apartment? Kill me? Kidnap me? What?"

"Heck, if the KGB wanted to kill you they would have long ago arranged some kind of fatal traffic accident, or dropped a piano on your head while you were walking down the street. They certainly aren't going to kidnap you – hell, if they did that we would immediately kidnap five of their agents and that would be the start of a real war."

"No, I'm afraid what they have in mind for you is sex and more sex. Any kind you have ever dreamed of and some you haven't even imagined as possible, the kinkier the better, whatever you want they will be more than happy to give you – and it will all be filmed in living color. I'm afraid you are going to have to take one for the team. Man up and have a jolly good romp with Ursula and the chance to live out your darkest fantasies. Just be sure to ask for 8X10 inch glossies of all your activities. We will hang them up in an honored location at the Station as a tribute to your sacrifices."

"Seriously, what am I supposed to do?"

"I'm serious, you've been on my ass for months to make some progress in this investigation and this is the best thing that's happened so far. Go with the flow, as they used to say. Just play out this string and see where it leads us. I'm pretty sure it's going to lead to a blackmail attempt and I'd love to know who the blackmailer is going to be. Just act like a big stupid American lummox and enjoy playing the game for all it's worth. Isn't this what you really wanted to happen?"

Martin was right. I was getting desperate for something to move this whole STAPO mole hunt forward. He was also right in that this was exactly the kind of thing I had been secretly wanted to happen to me personally – to actually be right in the middle of an intelligence operation. I couldn't deny it; I was hooked on all these spy shenanigans. Here was my chance to really be a spy, and the only cost to me was to have crazy sex with a beautiful woman. What could I possibly complain about – this was a teenage fantasy come true.

"OK, you're right. I'll just take one for the team and screw my brains out for God and country."

"Good man, I knew you had that kind of raw courage inside of you. We're all proud of the sacrifices you're willing to make to keep American free," Martin said, and then burst out laughing so hard that I thought he would fall out of his chair.

"Just give me her name, address, and phone number. We'll start looking into whom young Ursula really is and try to learn everything about her and whom she consorts with. I sure as hell wish we could trust the STAPO; this kind of investigation is right up their alley. Well, I've still got a couple of Federal Police officers that I think I can trust to help out with this. In any case this is my problem. You need to focus on building up your body and taking lots of vitamins to help prepare for your coming weekend ordeal."

"You're really loving this, aren't you Martin?"

"Oh, you bet I am. Now you know why they say 'be careful what you wish for...'. You have absolutely made my day. This was well worth ruining my day's plans for the chance to see you squirm over this completely ridiculous situation you've gotten yourself into."

Well he was right and I had to admit it. Time to man up and stop whining!

For once, my week flew by. I now had something to occupy my mind with each day when I was alone in my office – imagining what was going to happen that weekend. All feelings of boredom had completely left me. I alternated between free-floating anxiety and sexual fantasies. What an absurd predicament to be in. The more I thought about it the more crazy it all seemed. My God, this was all too weird to be true.

On Thursday, Martin invited me into the Station for a briefing. He had the results of his initial look-see at my loving Ursula.

"She is definitely STASI. Did she tell you where she was from?"

"She said she was from Berlin."

"Well that's interesting. She actually told you the truth. She is from Berlin, but it's East Berlin. She's so young that we really don't have much on her other than that when she graduated from university she was picked up by the STASI and put into their swallow training program. She's already badly burned one British diplomat who was almost coerced into treason. He finally admitted all and was sent home in disgrace, but at least avoided becoming a traitor. Her real name is Lisa Koch."

"Okay..."

"Well, you wanted to know, and now you know. Are you going to be able to go through with this? We are going to keep her apartment under surveillance. As I told you before, I would personally be grief stricken if you so much as broke a fingernail while tussling with the KGB, or even the STASI. Or with Lisa, AKA Ursula."

"Yes, I'm going to go through with it. I'm just not sure what I'm willing to do to become blackmailable. This whole fiasco is actually starting to turn my stomach."

"Look, let me be serious with you for once. You don't have to do this at all. You can just not show up. We can report Lisa to the STAPO as an East German illegal and get her arrested and/or thrown out of the country. I can't imagine any moles sticking their necks out to save her. We won't have lost anything, and who knows it might even prod the KGB into trying something else even more stupid. I realize that all of this is really seriously weird and sick and very uncomfortable for you. I've joked around with you a lot about this, but I honestly don't know what I would do in your place. I'd probably not show up, but of course I'm married and this would be hell on my wife. Maybe you have less to lose, but again, I understand just how uncomfortable this all must be for you. Who knows what weird stuff they have in mind for setting you up for blackmail? Just say the word and I'll drop a dime on her to the STAPO right now."

"No, I'm just being a wimp. I'll do the best I can and see what comes from it, but thanks for understanding that it's seriously messing with my mind."

"No problem, remember we'll be watching the apartment and if any shit hits the fan just bail out of there. Oh, and for God's sake, just for once - don't bring that damned pistol with you. I don't want anybody shot with it, especially not you!"

So, like a condemned man, I counted down the hours until 8:00 PM Friday night. When the time drew near, I took the U-Bahn to her apartment. I didn't want to be encumbered by my car. I had a small case with me containing toiletries and clothes for my fun weekend.

Her apartment was on the top floor of the building, and it had a modern elevator. I rode it up to her floor and knocked. She opened the door almost instantly, gave me a big hug and kiss and led me into her apartment. It was a large and modern two-bedroom unit, actually a little bigger than mine. Not the kind of place I expected a university student to be living in. We walked into an expansive, comfortable living room with very modern Scandinavian-style furniture in it. I was surprised to find another woman sitting there. Lisa, oops, I mean Ursula, introduced her to me as Heinriette. Heinriette was also very attractive, but strikingly different from Ursula. She was quite tall, I think over six feet in height, and older, probably in her early thirties. She had light brown hair worn very long and wavy down her back. She looked more like a fashion model than a student. She wore a high-fashion little black dress.

Ursula said, "Heinriette is also German and one of my oldest and dearest friends. She is the executive assistant to the president of a large plastics company and she pays most of our rent. She's a real dear and I know you'll like her as much as you do me."

Heinriette stood, smiled, walked over to me, and shook my hand. "Ursula has told me what a wonderfully nice man you are, Stephen, and I'm very happy to meet you." Heinriette's accent was considerably thicker than Ursula's, but she still spoke English quite well.

Ursula then pointed to another room and said, "Please put your bag into my bedroom and come back and have a drink with us. Heinriette has been dying to speak with you."

I did as told and soon sat down on the couch with Ursula. Heinriette sat opposite us in an expensive looking leather chair. Ursula got up to fetch the promised drink and Heinriette said, "Stephen, tell me all about yourself. Ursula tells me you work here in Vienna. Where?"

"I work at the US Embassy."

"Ah, so you are an American diplomat?"

"No, I work for the US government, but not as a diplomat."

Heinriette looked quizzically at me, smiled, and said, "Oh, is it a secret? You're not a spy, are you?"

"Nothing so romantic." Then Ursula appeared with a drink for me. I was extremely nervous and so I gulped it down very quickly. I don't even remember what it was, other than it contained alcohol.

Ursula looked surprised and then said, "My Stephen, you must be thirsty. Would you like another drink?"

"Yes, please." I really needed something to steady my nerves. It was crazy, I know, but I was extremely nervous. No, that's not true, I was scared. In spite of all that Martin had said to me I really felt I was in an extremely dangerous situation and I was really wishing I had never shown up here. I had visions of waking up tomorrow lying next to Ursula's dead body, or something equally gruesome that could serve as grist for a very serious blackmail attempt against me. Well, it was way too late for regrets.

Ursula came back with another drink and I drank this one much more slowly. It seemed to be some kind of sweet liqueur and didn't taste bad at all. Also, I was now starting to relax. The alcohol must have been calming me down. What was I so afraid of, really? Two beautiful women here, probably at my beck and call, and I'm nervous? I actually burst out laughing at how ridiculous the whole situation was. I was startled to suddenly find myself laughing so loudly, and that actually made it all seem even funnier. I laughed until my stomach actually hurt. The situation I was in was all so funny!

Heinriette then stood and said something to Ursula in German. Then they both came over to me and lifted me up by my arms. For some reason, my legs weren't working very well, but everything was going to be OK because these beautiful women were now helping me. They were so kind and so beautiful I felt lucky to have them as my friends. They guided and then half carried me into a bedroom. There they started to take my clothes off and it was very hard not to be ticklish. I tried to tell them that it was OK because I didn't have my pistol in my pants pocket, but somehow when I tried to speak it all sounded garbled to me. I realized they couldn't understand me and that made me very sad. I started crying because of this overwhelming sadness and then suddenly everything went black.

17

THE SHIT HITS THE FAN

I woke up at the bottom of a very deep well. My head hurt and I felt sick to my stomach. I was looking up the well to its top and seeing an extremely bright light way up there. It must have been the sun. I then felt very tired and weak and decided to close my eyes and sleep for a while longer.

The next time I woke up I realized that I wasn't in a well, but in a room. I thought it was the same room those beautiful women had helped me into. I turned my head, and sure enough I was lying on a bed. I still had a sick headache but I seemed to be able to move a little better now. The light in the ceiling over the bed was very bright and hurt my eyes, so I closed them and fell asleep again.

The last time I woke up, my head was positively pounding and I felt very sick to my stomach. I needed to find a bathroom in which to throw up. I got out of bed and looked around, saw an open bathroom door and lurched into it. I threw up absolutely everything in my stomach and continued on right through the dry heaves. Finally, my retching stopped and I got up shakily and lurched over to the bathroom sink. I splashed water on my face and cleaned it off as best as I could. I stood up, looked in the mirror and noticed that I was completely naked. I also had terrible scratches on my chest that were bleeding a little. Man, what had happened to me? Where was I? I vaguely remembered beautiful women, but looked around and didn't see anyone.

I called out: "Hey, is anyone here?" No answer came. I went back into the room and saw my clothes piled on the floor. I very slowly and carefully dressed myself. When I bent over to pick up my clothes my head really started to spin, so I had to move very slowly. I felt extremely clumsy and had a very hard time buttoning my shirt. Getting my pants on was a little easier. Then I saw my small case on the floor by the bedroom door. That helped me remember where I was: Ursula's apartment!

Where were Ursula and Heinriette? What time was it? What had happened to me? Was I having a stroke? Had they gone for medical aid? No, that didn't make sense, they would have stayed with me and called for an ambulance on the phone. Where the hell were they? I needed medical help. It looked like I was going to need to get it myself, no one was here to help.

I picked up my case and staggered out of the bedroom. Ah, I remember this living room. I remember where the front door is. I called out again: "Anyone here?"

No answer, so I made my way weaving to the front door. I turned the knob and it opened. I remembered where the elevator was and made my way slowly and unsteadily to it. I pushed the down button, waited what seemed like hours, and finally the elevator doors very slowly opened. I looked inside expecting to see Ursula and Heinriette, but the elevator was empty. The walls of the elevator seemed to be moving in and out and its floor had colored waves of light moving across it. I staggered inside, pressed the button for the ground floor, and closed my eyes. I felt like I was going to pass out, but eventually the elevator jerked to a stop and I heard the doors open again. When I opened my eyes I almost fell into the lobby, but caught myself just in time. I slowly crept through the empty lobby, which now seemed to be miles long, and finally came to the lobby doors. It took all my strength to push one open, but I managed it and was now outside on the top of steps leading down to the sidewalk. The steps were moving back and forth quite violently and I knew I would fall if I tried to walk down them. So, I just sat down on the top step and started to cry. I was going to die of a stroke, the world was going mad, and no one was there to help me.

I sat crying on the top step, when suddenly a man appeared next to me and said, "Stephen!" I looked at him and said: "I have to get to a hospital." Soon another man joined the first man, and a car screeched to a halt in front of the building. The two men helped me into the back seat of the car and it drove off. I was completely exhausted and so fell asleep again.

I woke up in a bed again, this time in another room. There was someone trying to pry my eyelid open and shine a bright light into it, which was the last thing I wanted right now. I yelled at him: "Leave me alone!" He backed away. It seemly took all my strength, but I managed to get both eyes open. I saw someone I knew in the room – it was Martin! I cried out: "Martin, help me, I'm dying!"

Martin came over to me and said, "No, Stephen, you aren't dying. You've been drugged. You're going to be OK. This man is a doctor and he's going to give you a shot that should make you feel much better very quickly. Just let him do that so that you can feel better, OK? You've been fighting everyone who has tried to touch you."

That sounded crazy to me. How could I have been fighting anyone when I was asleep? However, I trusted Martin and croaked, "OK."

The man Martin said was a doctor rolled up my sleeve, dabbed alcohol on my arm, and stuck a needle into it. I normally don't like shots and never look at the needle going in, but this time for some reason I wanted to really see it happen. I then heard a roaring sound in my ears and fell asleep again.

When I next woke up, I felt almost normal again. I had been in a deep sleep with some very crazy dreams. I had dreamt that I had been in a crazy apartment building with two beautiful women and that I had a stroke. I opened my eyes fully and found myself in a familiar bedroom. The man that Martin said was a doctor was sitting in a chair reading a newspaper. I said: "Doctor, I'm thirsty."

He immediately bounded out of his chair, opened the room's door and shouted: "He's awake!"

With that a whole bunch of people, including Martin, entered the room. They all looked very happy to see me. I sat up in bed, and found that my head now only hurt a little. I sipped from a glass of water one of the men handed to me.

Martin said, "Stephen, I'm so happy to see you're OK. You had me really worried. I thought you'd broken a lot more than a fingernail. What the hell happened to you in that apartment? Where are the women who were there?"

I told Martin everything I remembered – coming to the apartment, seeing Ursula and Heinriette, having a couple of drinks, being carried into a bedroom, and then feeling like I had a stroke.

"So, that's all you remember? You don't know what happened to the women?"

"No, the only other things I remember are waking up in a bedroom, feeling very sick, having a very hard time getting dressed, and having a real struggle getting out of the building. What did happen? What time is it?"

Martin said: "Right now it's about 9:30 AM Saturday. You've lost over half a day. They drugged you. When my team noticed you sitting on the apartment house steps crying, everyone freaked out, but they managed to get you here safely without attracting much attention and then get you the medical help you needed. My God, you scared the crap out of me!"

"We immediately sent part of the team to the apartment to check it out. I'll need to contact the team members soon to find out what's happening there. I've been completely tied up here waiting to see if you were going to be all right. Anyway, that's really all you remember?"

"That's all."

"All right, you're in a safe house now and you need to rest up. The doc here says that you been pumped full of God knows what kinds of drugs. He's treated you for barbiturate poisoning and that seems to have helped your condition quite a bit."

"It's so nice to know you cared." I said, and laughed when Martin suddenly looked shocked at what I had just said. He then realized I had actually made a feeble joke and joined in on the laughing and slapped me on the back.

"I think it's time for you to go home. I have no idea what they did to you last night and I think the best bet would be to put you on a plane back to the US."

"No," I shouted. "I haven't gone through all this shit just to bail out. What about the blackmail attempt? How are we going to learn anything if I just disappear from Austria? Then everything I've gone through will be a complete waste of time. I am not going home!"

Martin thought for a moment, and then said, "OK, but in that case you're going to a military hospital in West Germany right away. We're putting you on an Air Force plane that's waiting at the Vienna Airport. It's about a two-hour flight to Ramstein Air Force Base where they've got a top of the line hospital. As soon as you feel fit enough to leave, you'll be on your way there immediately. You've got to get a complete medical checkup, and it can't be done here in Austria without the STAPO finding out. Understand?"

"Yeah, let's go right now." I stood up a little wobbly, but headed for the door. Martin called out through the door: "Get the car, we're going now."

Martin had magically acquired a diplomatic passport in my name and he and the other two members of his team already had diplomatic cover, so we all zipped through Austrian immigration and customs formalities very quickly. We boarded an Air Force C-141 Starlifter that we had all to ourselves. As soon as we were on board, the plane was buttoned up, the engines started, and we were taxiing towards the runway. I was still feeling exhausted and feel asleep in my seat. I woke again as the aircraft bounced on the landing strip of Ramstein Air Force Base.

We taxied for a few minutes and stopped on an apron where an Air Force ambulance stood. I was actually feeling a lot better by now and stepped off the plane and into the ambulance without any assistance. As soon as I was lying down in the back of the ambulance it zoomed off with siren wailing and headed for the Landstuhl Army Medical Center, less than 5 miles away from the base. I think we broke all speed records getting there. We pulled up to the emergency entrance and I was quickly wheeled up to a private room where doctors and nurses galore awaited me.

I was undressed, poked and prodded, had copious amounts of blood drawn, was X-rayed, had my reflexes tested, and was even interviewed by a shrink. After all that was over it was pretty late in the evening, and I was feeling very tired again, when Martin came into my room. He looked extremely happy.

"Stephen, you're not going to believe what those chuckle-head STASI agents did? Apparently they left you alone in the room unguarded and went off to get a film crew and some supporting cast members for your great performance. I guess the scratching you got on your chest was just foreplay. When the whole crew finally returned with cameras and lights in hand, they found that you had mysteriously vanished. The team we sent in to check out the apartment got out just in time right before they all arrived, but were able to monitor everything that happened next."

"Apparently the girls, the film crew, and the supporting cast tore the apartment apart looking for you and there was some real screaming and yelling going on after that. It got so loud that the neighbors ended up calling the police. When the police showed up they got a little suspicions of all the people and the cameras and lights. Then they noticed that some blood was on the bed, likely from your chest scratches. They started thinking that they had busted some kind of a porno film operation, maybe even one making a snuff film. So, they were just about to haul the entire group off to the pokey, when guess who arrived to smooth everything out?"

"Who?"

"Why your good friend, Nico, that's who. Apparently he spent almost two hours there pulling strings to get the eager officers to back off and let everyone go. So, you missed out on your opportunity to be blackmailed by taking a powder at a most inopportune moment. Yet, it all worked out in the end because we now have clear proof that Nico is a very bad boy, indeed. The only thing left to determine is whether his boss Dr. Dorn is a willing co-conspirator or is just being played for a patsy by Nico. So, in spite of your not ending up having the wildest sexual experience of your entire life, you've managed, by sheerest luck and complete blundering, to have given us the first real evidence of at least one mole in STAPO. Congratulations, and my commiserations to you on your loss of one hot young girlfriend."

"Gee, thanks Martin."

"Hey, you still look like hell, I'm sorry I disturbed you so late in the evening, but I knew you would want to hear about what finally went down. So far the doctors have determined that you were fed some kind of crazy cocktail of downers, psychoactive drugs, and even a hallucinogen or two. The drugs seem to all be leaving your system now without causing any permanent brain damage, other than what you already had."

"You must have the constitution of an ox to have gotten out of that apartment with all those drugs in you. Hell, you even brought your damned bag out with you. The doctors all say it should have been impossible for you to do that. I've really underestimated you, and more importantly, so did the KGB. So sleep tight, my little man. You are the luckiest son of a bitch I've ever met and we owe you big time!"

I ended up spending the entire next day in the hospital under extremely close observation. I ate like a horse and drank gallons of water and by the following day was raring to get out of there and back to Vienna and re-engage in battle. Martin visited me and said that he wanted me to participate in all future daily briefings regarding Nico and the KGB penetration of STAPO, so I guess I had just been asked to join the "boy's club". Things were looked up for me. I was actually being taken seriously as more than just a "staked goat" by the head of the Vienna CIA Station. Not bad for a computer nerd! I was feeling on top of the world.

Things, however, were not so happy for Nico. Everything that seemed good for me was very bad for him. He was starting to get the feeling that the rats were closing in on him. That damned Stephen Connor was like a piece of gum stuck to his shoe, and one he couldn't scrape off. It was time to take care of me once and for all. He was incredibly disappointed in how badly the KGB had tried to deal with me and he was going to correct their mistake. It was so, so simple. All he had to do was kill me!

Nico was primarily a bully. He had grown up in Vienna during the Soviet occupation. He lived in the part of Vienna that fell within the Soviet sector. He quickly realized that of all the occupying powers in Austria – the Soviet Union, US, France, and Great Britain – only the Soviets seemed to grasp the true usefulness of power. The other nations were too soft and too weak in their basic character. Only the Soviets seemed to understand that the exertion of raw naked power was the best way to get what you wanted.

Nico wasn't a Communist. He was actually a Fascist who greatly admired Hitler, but the Soviets were the one nation that seemed to act as he felt a nation should act. He would hitch his star to them and use them to get the power he dreamed of, and which he felt he so richly deserved. He actually dreamed of ruling a new and even more powerful Austro-Hungarian Empire someday. Then the Soviets who had treated him like a lackey would finally recognize that he was a true vital force of nature to be respected and feared. The tables would be turned and they would finally realize that instead of using him, he had used them to gain ultimate power. In more simple terms, Nico was a psychopath.

He was also aware of the fatwa that had been issued and which called for my death. He even had a copy made of it and kept in his safe. He would use it to deflect blame for my death onto the Iranians. It would all work out so beautifully. Even his KGB handler wouldn't know for sure who had killed me. One day, the right day, he would tell them how he had cleaned up their mess single-handedly and they would come to admire him for his determination to let nothing stand in his way.

It was easy for him to get hold of an AK-47, the weapon of choice for Middle Eastern fanatics. He would dress like one so that if seen killing me, witnesses would report that it was a Middle Eastern terrorist who had executed me. He would carefully steer the STAPO investigation so that it came to the same conclusion. Dr. Dorn was a senile old fool who had become more and more easily manipulated over time. It would all be so easy to do; yet the KGB had apparently failed to grasp the utter simplicity and beauty of this idea. He was saddled by having to work with idiots, but he would not let that hold him back.

18

MY TRIUMPHANT RETURN

In early March 1980 I finally returned to Vienna after nearly a week in the Army Hospital. The staff there seemed to just want to draw more and more blood and run test after test on me. They were completely fascinated by all of the drugs that I had been given and what their final effect might be on my mind and body. I was afraid they would end up keeping me there as a permanent mascot, but I was eventually sprung by Martin. When he did, he also told me that Lisa and her friend had completely vanished, along with the camera crew and the others. No one seemed to have a clue as to what happened to them, but their complete disappearance had Nico's fingerprints all over it.

Spring was just around the corner and Vienna was shaking off the effects of a particularly harsh winter. When I got back to my apartment, I got my Sig P230 out of its locked case, cleaned and checked it out, and put it back into its pocket holster located in my right front pants pocket. A spare magazine went into my left rear pocket. I had felt somewhat naked without my little pistol; it had become such a habit for me to have it with me at all times. I vowed to myself to get in some practice time at the commercial pistol range located in the Liesing district of Vienna, and not very far from Hietzing. It had been far too long since I had fired it and I clearly recalled what I had been told about handgun skills being perishable.

My first day back at my Embassy office was a real pleasure. Martin immediately called me back into the Station, and I'll be damned if he didn't have a cake there to help celebrate my return. The cake had been decorated with a rather vulgar scene featuring a naked woman with short blonde hair. I had no idea where he could of gotten that monstrosity created. The cake was extremely delicious, though, as was expected of any baked goods that could be found in

Vienna.

Martin then took me back to a conference room where a team of his officers quickly assembled.

"Guys, this is the infamous Stephen Connor, the luckiest man in the world. He's not very bright, but this man has a natural talent for getting into and out from the most insane scrapes imaginable. I've decided to make him part of the STAPO penetration team and you should treat him just as you would any other member of the group."

After that stirring introduction, there was polite applause and even some backslapping and handshaking by the team members. Martin then continued: "We're going to use his luck, and maybe tap into his amazing constitution, in order to finally wrap up this question: in addition to Nico, are there any more moles in STAPO? After we've answered that question, we are going to squeeze those rats for all they've got and see if we can't double them. Langley really, really, wants us to be able to use them as double agents against the Soviets. If we can pull that off, we will all be heroes and be showered with huge bonuses and accolades. Well, maybe not any bonuses." Everyone laughed at the reference to the notorious stinginess of the CIA.

"We're going to make the most use we can of the 'luckiest man in the world' to pull this off. The first thing we are going to do is to send our hero off into the lion's den today. He's going to personally deliver a big pile of background check requests to our favorite swine, Nico, and see if he can't get a rise out of him."

More laughter and applause broke out. Martin motioned for silence.

"Now, Stephen: I want you to be as abrasive and as obnoxious as only you can be to our friend Nico. I want you to do anything you can, short of spitting in his face, to demonstrate a complete contempt for him. I want you to make clear just how little you think of him and that you are fully aware of what a lying, thieving, traitor he is. Don't come right out and say it, but do all you can to otherwise make it clear that you think he is a jackal and a swine and that he's about to take a big fall. Really piss him off, as only you can do so well. You up for it?"

"Hell, yes!" More applause and cheering ensued, this time loud and long.

Martin then struggled to regain control of the raucous group, grabbed up a file folder and said to me, "All right then, here are your background check requests. Go forth and rattle the cage of the jackal!"

I took all of the background check documents and marched off to see Nico. I walked to the U3 U-Bahn station and took the short ride to the Ministry of

Interior building. The guards at the lobby desk were very used to me by now, so they just handed me my visitor's badge and wished me a good morning. I marched up the stairs to the third floor and down the hall to Nico's office.

His door was closed but I didn't even bother to knock. I just threw open the door so that it banged against the wall and strolled right in like I owned the place. I saw Nico jerk up his head from reading some documents on his desk.

"Hey, Nico, how are things in the wonderful world of secretaries? Typed up anything hot today? Met any cute blondes? Say, do you like college students or are they too young for you?"

Nico's face turned beet red. I thought he was the one who was actually going to have a stroke today. He stuttered and stammered in fury, unable to speak.

"What's the matter, cat got your tongue? Hey, can you put a rush on these applications for me? I've got a busy few days ahead of me. I've really become interested in the architecture of Vienna and I want to spend more time looking over all of the beautiful palaces you have here. So, if you can use your admirable paper-pushing skills, I'd really appreciate it. Say, what do all you secretaries talk about during your breaks? Fashion, hair styles, strategies for raising kids?"

Nico suddenly stood up and started moving towards me quite aggressively. I suddenly got the feeling I may have gone too far in taunting him. I set my feet and moved my body into a position to deliver a two-handed palm strike to his head, just like I'd learned in my Directorate of Security training. I fully expected that I would have to hit him. Just then, the intercom on his desk buzzed and I heard the voice of Dr. Dorn calling: "Nico?"

Nico froze in mid-stride. This was too good to be true, so I took one more shot at Nico's ego and said: "Sorry we can't dance right now, but it looks like your master is calling."

With that I turned on my heels, walked out the doorway, and slammed his door shut. I thought that Martin would have been very proud of my performance in "poking the bear".

After Nico had dealt with Dr. Dorn's request, he sat back down at his desk and began quite happily planning my death for that very night.

I returned to the Embassy and briefed the team on my Nico taunting. They absolutely roared in laughter and made me repeat everything I said to Nico three times. They also wanted me to demonstrate the two-handed palm strike I had planned to use on him. During my demonstration I hit one of the team members, George, in the chest so hard with it that it actually knocked him off his feet.

More laughter then ensured and everyone eventually left the conference room in a state of high hilarity.

I spent most of the rest of the day in the Station brainstorming with Martin and the other team members on how to finally determine if Dr. Dorn were a mole or a dupe. Other than keeping him under constant surveillance to see if he ever had contact with the KGB, no one seemed to have any great ideas on just how to do that. We did kick around the idea of somehow feeding him some really juicy information about CIA activities in Vienna and then seeing if the KGB acted upon it, but there was always the possibility that he might just tell Nico about the information and the KGB could get it that way. What to do, what to do?

I finally headed home around 6:00 PM. As usual, I rode the U3 to my streetcar line, and then rode it down the Hietzinger Haupstrasse to my stop. I got off the streetcar and walked to my apartment.

I put together a small dinner for myself and ate it in my kitchen. I then turned on the TV and started watching "The Rockford Files". Of course, Austrian Television had dubbed it into German, but I had loved this show in the US, knew most of the episodes, and was actually using it to help me learn more German. After the show was over, I put Armed Forces Radio on my shortwave radio and listened to the news and the latest American music. AFR was a godsend for Americans in Europe as they had powerful broadcasting stations all over West Germany. One station was in Bavaria not far from the Austrian border and it came in on my radio very clearly. AFR had great news and music programs. Around 9:00 PM I was sitting on my living room couch reading a book and listening to music on the radio when my doorbell rang.

I got up to see who it was. When I opened the door, I saw a very strange sight – Nico wearing some outrageous Middle Eastern costume and pointing an AK-47 at me. He shoved the weapon into my stomach in order to push me back into my apartment.

That was a huge mistake. Nico was way over confident that the sight of a military rifle would turn me into a helpless mass of Jello begging for my life. He should have shot me the very moment I opened the door. What happened instead was that I quickly stepped back, grabbed the barrel of the AK-47 with my left hand and drew it around my left side. This pulled Nico into me, and now the barrel of the rifle was no longer pointing at me. I had trained with this very scenario many times at the CIA's Directorate of Security Training Center. Even though it had been many months since I had practiced it, I didn't even have to think about what to do in this situation. I reacted completely automatically.

Everything then suddenly seemed to go into slow motion and my hearing even seemed to shut down. I barely heard the rifle go off, harmlessly blowing holes in my living room wall. Nico was now trying to step away from me and attempting to yank the AK-47 back so that he could get it pointed at me again. However, at the same time he was doing that, I was reaching into my pocket with my right hand and pulling out my little Sig P230. We were still quite close together so I was able to very quickly get the pistol clear of my pocket, rotate it forward, angle the slide away from my body so it wouldn't catch on any clothing, and without even looking at it point the pistol towards Nico's left hip and fire it.

I was looking right into Nico's eyes when he first realized that he had been shot. He was definitely hurting, as his pelvis had been partially fractured by my bullet. This meant that he could no longer put any weight on his left leg and he was starting to fall backwards. Yet I didn't see any fear at all in his eyes, just hatred and a strange sense of confidence. He still thought he was going to kill me.

As he started to fall, the distance between us slowly grew. I was still able to hold the AK-47's barrel off to my left side and I was just starting to notice the heat coming from it. Nico was still firing it and bullets were chewing up my living room very badly. When Nico's head was far enough away from me to raise my Sig up to its level, I did just that and fired an aimed shot right into his left eye. It destroyed the eye completely and the bullet ripped deeply into his brain. His remaining right eye seemed to show real surprise for the briefest of moments and then the life in it somehow just went out. It really did look like a doll eye now as he continued falling. I shot him one more time in the forehead as he was going down to the floor. Nico's skull was hard enough to stop this bullet, and although it slightly fractured his skull, that bullet didn't penetrate into his brain. The CIA had taught me that with a pistol you keep shooting until you are sure the threat has stopped. Pistol bullets are pretty anemic compared to rifle bullets and it usually will take multiple hits to stop an attacker. In fact, the vast majority of pistol gunshot victims survive their shootings, but Nico wasn't going to - not with a hollow-point bullet deep in his brain.

I stood over Nico's body looking down at it and realized I was still holding a very hot AK-47 barrel in my left hand. I put the AK down on the floor. I had been experiencing such tunnel vision that I hadn't even looked beyond Nico the entire time we were fighting to see if he had any accomplices. If he had, I would probably have been dead, but after I scanned the hallway it appeared as though he had been alone.

I ejected the partially depleted magazine from my Sig and inserted the spare full magazine I kept in my back pocket. I did this so that I would have a full magazine in my pistol if any friends of Nico did actually show up.

What with all the shooting that had just occurred, the police were bound to arrive soon, so I put the Sig back into its pocket holster in my pants pocket. I didn't want to get accidentally shot by them. Police handling a "shots fired" call tend to see anyone with a gun in their hand as the bad guy. I stepped back from the door and walked to my phone. I picked it up and dialed the emergency number for the CIA Station. The duty officer picked up on the first ring and I briefed him on what had just happened. He told me to sit tight, say as little as possible to the Austrian police, and wait for the cavalry to arrive.

When the first two Federal Police officers arrived, they were cautious but polite. They had no idea who the dead man was and he did look to be dressed like some kind of crazy terrorist. They asked me where my gun was and I told them it was in my pocket. They had me raise my hands and turn around, and then one of them carefully removed the pistol from its pocket holster. While I was in that position he also patted me down thoroughly for any other weapons. They radioed for an ambulance, even though Nico was well beyond needing one. They then had me sit down on my couch and started asking me exactly what happened, who I was, and did I know the dead guy who was lying in the hallway.

I told them that this man had tried to kill me and that I was still extremely upset and confused. I said I would be happy to file an official complaint against him for attempted murder but that I was feeling very unwell now and wanted a doctor. I then closed my eyes and slumped back on the couch. This got them to stop asking questions and start radioing for another ambulance. It would buy me more than enough time for a support team, including legal counsel, to arrive from the Embassy. After closing my eyes I realized that I actually was feeling completely spent. So, I just sat there with my eyes closed until the ambulance arrived, immediately followed by the first of the Embassy cavalry. I also, however, felt like it had been the very best day of my life. I had never felt more alive than at that very moment. I had put my life on the line and I had won. I really was going to love being a spy.

19

EPILOGUE

I ended up spending a day at the hospital, even being handcuffed to the bed for a short time while the Federal Police tried to sort out just what the heck had happened. It was a complete mystery to them. I had obviously shot one of their own, but he had completely shot up my apartment with an AK-47 and was wearing bizarre clothing. There was simply no way to explain his behavior as being in any way lawful. They couldn't make head or tails of it. They eventually gave up, and did their best to just completely cover up the fact that the mad terrorist who had been killed in Hietzing was actually a member of STAPO. They finally decided that I had actually acted in self-defense and in turn I agreed not to discuss the incident with the press.

Dr. Dorn had to resign, officially due to health reasons, but he was definitely done at STAPO. There was a big shake up there, and the new STAPO Director, Dr. Manz, actually made some very discreet moves to improve relations with the local CIA Station. STAPO would shortly thereafter become a lot more effective in controlling any excesses of the KGB in Austria. Our best guess is that Dr. Dorn was a dupe of Nico's, but I think we'll never be sure as to his exact involvement with the KGB's penetration of STAPO.

Franz continued on as Chief of Police of Bregenz, where he did a brilliant job. He would end up being promoted again and made the Chief of Police of the entire surrounding state of Vorarlberg. He purchased the home he had been renting when I first visited him and still very happily lives there. I visited with Franz, Lena, and the children many times during my stay in Austria and they will always feel like family to me.

There was a huge shakeup of the KGB Residence in Vienna after Nico's death, although no blame was ever officially attributed to them for Nico's bizarre behavior. All of his misdeeds were buried with him in his grave. The local KGB Resident was replaced and his career was effectively ended. One bit of good news for them, though, was that the KGB soon came to the realization that Nico had been the only target of their nemesis Stephen Connor. Nico's loss was a bitter blow to them, but their really important agent, Jonas Bauer, appeared to be completely in the clear. So, when dust finally settled after Nico's death, my old KGB friend Viktor Avilov reactivated Harri Aalto as Jonas' controller and the whole operation continued on as originally planned.

Jonas went on to have a wonderful career with both the KGB and the State Department. He eventually was promoted to Deputy Chief of Station, the number two person in the US Embassy in Vienna, and provided a huge amount of vital intelligence to the Soviet Union for many years. There is reason to believe that he was the KGB's most highly paid agent ever, some indication of how greatly they valued him. He was never suspected of any misdeeds while serving at the Embassy, only being caught after he left it for a promotion to an even loftier position in Washington, DC. It was actually the FBI who finally caught him, rather than CIA counter-intelligence. I certainly regret that I never suspected Jonas for even one minute while I was working at the Embassy.

As for me – well all my dreams came true. Martin officially requested that I be transferred from the Directorate of Intelligence to the Directorate of Operations and be assigned to the Vienna Station. Although Langley was clearly disappointed about not being able to turn anyone into a double agent, the request was quickly approved. This, in turn, resulted in Langley ordering me to return to the US to receive the necessary training required for any new employee of the Directorate of Operations. Martin firmly resisted this request. He said that I had already demonstrated all of the necessary skills that any CIA clandestine officer needed to have and that he frankly couldn't spare me from the vital work I was already doing in Vienna. Apparently it was actually my good old friend in Langley, the Deputy Director of Intelligence, who threw his weight behind this request and finally got a training exemption pushed through for approval. I still wonder whether he did it because he felt grateful to me or if he was just trying to make sure that I was completely out of his Directorate as quickly as possible. I guess I'll never know for sure.

I never did get my little Sig P230 back from the Austrian Federal Police, and ended up replacing it while I was in Vienna with a Walther PPK. Yes, just like James Bond!

I stayed on at the Vienna Station until June of 1982. After that I was transferred out of Vienna to a new assignment – one beyond the scope of this book. During my later years in Vienna I never really worked on anything as exciting as the STAPO mole hunt, and never had to kill anyone else, but I think I did some good work there, nevertheless. I know that Martin and I are still great friends and he still calls me "the luckiest man in the world".

The KGB still continued to watch me extremely closely and always considered me to be some kind of super agent while I was with the CIA. If anything, my killing Nico only raised their opinion of me. They never did figure out that I just had the uncanny ability to accidentally get myself into the craziest situations conceivable. If nothing else, I succeeded in getting them to waste tremendous resources in trying to determine what I was up to. Anywhere I went they almost always panicked and often suspended viable operations while I was around. It's a good feeling to know that I was such a pain in their butts.

I eventually left the CIA and ended up taking a job at the Naval Surface Warfare Center. I guess I finally got tired of working in the hall of mirrors. However, after only few years with the Navy, I again got fed up with working within the restrictions of such a highly classified military environment and finally left government service entirely to become a consultant.

Of course, my very first consulting client ended up being the NSA! Nevertheless, I eventually took on business clients and consulting was a very good career for me. It took me all over the world. I traveled about forty weeks out of every year and soon realized I could live anywhere in the eastern US where there was an airport. So, I ended up moving to the little college town of Huntington, West Virginia. There I met my lovely wife and there is where I recently retired from consulting.

The Iranian arrest warrant and fatwa against me have never been rescinded and so I'm still remaining somewhat vigilant about them, but probably needlessly so. I wonder if the Iranian revolutionaries still care about what happens to a man as old as I am. Well, I guess you can never really know how long they might want to carry a grudge.

I finally took the advice that was given to me so many years ago by that firearms instructor at The Farm, and actually started shooting in Practical Pistol competitions. I recently competed in the Kentucky Handgun Championship and acquitted myself fairly well there. I can still shoot a handgun very accurately. I have a concealed carry permit and still carry a pistol with me at all times in a pocket holster. Only today, it's a Sig P290RS in 9mm.

Oh, and I'm still the luckiest man in the world. I have wonderful friends, live in a lovely little town, have the best wife in the world and an extended family consisting of her terrific kids and grand kids. What more could a man ever wish for? Just how lucky can a man get?

ABOUT THE AUTHOR

Michael Connick has based this novel on his real life experiences working with the intelligence community, the Department of Defense, and the technology industry. Michael was born and raised in San Francisco, served as a consultant to the SAVAK in Tehran, and worked and lived in Vienna, Austria. He now resides in Huntington, WV, where he writes, competes in Practical Pistol shooting competitions, volunteers with local organizations, and is very happily married to a truly wonderful wife.

Made in United States
North Haven, CT
05 May 2024